INSANITY

INSANITY

PETER BARRY

BLACKFOREST
PUBLICATIONS

INSANITY

First published in 2020 by
Blackforest Publications
36 Woodlea Court
Woodend
VIC. 3442
Australia.

ISBN: 9780646825106

I Hate Martin Amis et al

We All Fall Down

The Walk

For Elizabeth

It's not a padded cell. That makes it more bearable. If it was up to him, I'm sure he'd have wanted me to be locked up in a padded cell, probably have them throw away the key too. He can be like that, not one to forgive and forget easily. But maybe I've just been lucky, and padded cells have gone the way of straitjackets. Maybe they're considered too Victorian.

It's a secure facility though, he made sure of that. There are key pads by every door, the downstairs windows are all barred, the garden has surveillance cameras in every tree and bush, and is enclosed by a high brick wall, and the main gate can only be opened remotely by staff in the Reception-cum-office area. It's a discrete kind of security though, like a hotel – even if it's one where the guests aren't allowed to leave (until they've paid, ha ha ha!).

It could have been a hotel once upon a time. It has that feel about it. The furniture in the lounge has certainly seen better days: sagging armchairs with rips here and there, faded curtains, inferior prints on every wall – but you know all this already, of course. Although you probably don't know that there's a large spider's web in the corner above the water dispenser. There are plastic chairs in the dining-room, and worn carpets in the corridors. It's all very genteel. Granny (my mum's mum) used to live in a place like this, only it was her home.

Unlike a hotel, the staff don't wear uniforms – apart from the doctors who wear white coats. If you want my opinion (which you probably don't), it's kind of creepy the staff wearing normal clothes. It's like they're pretending to be who they're not, going about their business incognito. If you'll excuse me saying so, they're behaving very like the people they're supposed to be looking after.

The guests in this make-believe hotel are something else. You'll be used to them, of course, but for a *sane* person like myself (ha ha), they're pretty out there. I see people like them in the street sometimes, talking to themselves, throwing their arms around, ducking their heads and rolling their eyes like they're doing their best to avoid everyone else who's out and about. But the difference in here is that everyone's like that – they're all nuts.

Except me of course. Seriously, I can't imagine how you can think I'm the same as them. He must have persuaded you somehow, I guess. Told you I was nuts and got you to lock me up. He can be very persuasive. And he has enough money to convince anyone of anything if he sets his mind on it.

Maybe that's why you've asked me to put my thoughts down on paper every day, in the hope I'll prove beyond doubt that I'm mad – condemn myself with my own words, and so save you a bit of work. Fact is, I'm only doing this, writing this garbage, for exactly the opposite reason: to prove how sane I am – which you must be aware of anyway, my sanity, surely! – even though no one's done any tests on me since I got here. The only so-called treatment I'm getting right now is being forced to dick around in group therapy. Writing in a school exercise book is way better than being forced to discuss feelings in front of a bunch of spaced out losers. It also helps pass the time.

I try to avoid the others as much as possible, TBH. I prefer to spend time in the garden. I like the garden, despite the CCTV cameras. It's really quite large, with many winding, gravel paths and well-tended flower beds. It's a classy establishment, I suppose, much better than those state-run institutions I've heard about. I've probably got him to thank him for that, although I don't think I'm up to doing that right now – thanking him, that is. I walk for hours, or sit on one of the many seats scattered around the grounds, my favourite being beneath a giant old oak tree whose branches reach out in every direction over the grass. Fortunately, it's spring, and the temperature is perfect for wandering and thinking. Although on some days it can already be too hot.

I'm not sure this incarceration, or whatever you call it, is doing me much good though. My preoccupation – which everyone, yourself included, insists on calling an obsession – is the same as it was before I was admitted: rising temperatures, otherwise known as global warming. So, *while* I'm here – *locked up* in here – I've decided it's the perfect opportunity to ask someone like yourself, an expert, some questions that have been bugging me lately.

How can today's prime ministers and presidents live with themselves?

How do they manage to sleep at night?

What makes them get up in the morning?

Why don't they all slit their wrists?

That's enough to be going on with.

If anyone knows the answers to these questions, it would surely be someone in your profession. I mean, I've never been able to get my head around understanding the motivations of those in power, but shrinks are supposed to understand what makes people tick and stuff like that, so you of all people must surely be able to explain it to me.

I'm serious about these questions, Dr. Craig. I admit to climate change being a preoccupation of mine over the last year or two. The very first time I met you, I said as much: 'It totally freaks me out, the world coming to an end and stuff.'

Yes, I had a bit of a rant. Sorry about losing it like that, but when you're up against people who are so extreme – who deny climate change, not just irrationally, but absolutely – it's hard not to react yourself.

All I'm asking is for you to explain to me how these so-called leaders live with themselves knowing that they're responsible for their descendants – their own flesh and blood – not being able to live in our world.

And I'm not talking about their great-great-great grand-children, or anyone as distant as that. (Those generations won't ever be born, if you ask me.) No, I'm talking about their grandchildren, and if not them, then absolutely definitely about their great-grandchildren.

Those generations won't have any kind of life at all. Food and water will be scarce. Homes will be hard to come by. Jobs will disappear. Even fresh, breathable air will be at a premium. Blah, blah, blah.

The thing is, we can imagine how awful the future will be, so why can't those in power?

You must have an insight into such minds. As a psychiatrist, you can surely explain to me how these people are able to tuck their kids into bed at night and wish them happy dreams. Yeah sure, I realise the people at the top probably don't tuck their kids in at night. They're far too busy glad-handing the sycophants who surround them, knocking back the free champers and stuffing their faces with foie gras and fresh lobster to spend time with their kids. They're too preoccupied with letting their colleagues and the media know what a great job they're doing fucking up the country to waste time reading their kids bedtime stories.

When I was saying this to you, I could see you were listening to me all right, but you weren't reacting. You were just staring at me. I don't know what I expected, that being my first (and only) one-on-one session with you, but I didn't expect you to do nothing, to just sit there and stare at me.

I have to admit, apart from being kind of creepy, it kind of annoyed me, like it was you who was responsible for me ending up in here. That's when I thought, fuck it, and just let rip. Well, it's what you're paid for is the way I see it. You're paid to listen to people rant and rave. That's your job.

So… The way I see it, politicians will do anything to avoid reading their kids bedtime stories. Why? Because they're terrified their kids will ask them that really awkward question, that impossible-to-answer question that every parent dreads. They'll be praying that their sweet little son or daughter, pink scrubbed-clean faces resting on fluffy white pillows, won't look up at them and ask, 'Daddy, what did you do to mitigate the effects of global warming today?'

I remember using that word when I spoke to you. *Mitigate.* I was proud of doing that, although I'm not sure you spotted the irony behind it.

'What I think,' I said to you, 'is that those spineless, self-serving, prevaricating mummies and daddies will be on their knees next to their little kiddies' beds every night they're home, praying desperately that they'll be asked the much easier-to-answer question, "Daddy, where did I come from?"'

You actually smiled when I said that. I took this as an encouraging sign.

'If they do find time to put their kids to bed one night a week, or month or year, what on earth can they say to the fruits of their loins – Is that the right expression?'

But you didn't answer, as usual. (I'm beginning to catch on that you never answer questions.)

'Maybe they say something like, "Night, night, sleep tight, mummy and daddy love you – and don't worry yourself about tomorrow, darling, because tomorrow will almost certainly never happen."

'That doesn't sound like a normal parent though, not a loving parent. So how about, "Night, night, sleep tight, mummy and daddy love you, even though we're leaving you with a world that's in a far worse state than the one we ourselves inherited". How about that, Dr. Craig?

'It's better, even though it's hardly what you'd call a reassuring or comforting message for a kid about to depart for noddy land.

'I prefer to think they don't say anything at all to their offspring at bedtime, because even politicians would be hard pressed to spin such an enormous lie, to be so two-faced in front of their own innocent flesh and blood. Surely they'd refuse to tell their children that they aren't going to enjoy any kind of future at all because daddy – or, let's not be sexist here, mummy – didn't do anything at all at work today to stop the build-up of greenhouse gas emissions. Surely even a politician would have the decency to remain silent?'

While I was saying this to you, I was thinking about the philosopher, or maybe writer, who said something about life or existence being short and brutish – like stamping on someone's face for all eternity. Or was it two different people who said different parts of that? Whatever. It's certainly going to be even more true in the future. With every year that passes life is going to get both shorter and more brutish, and there'll be even more stamping on faces.

I didn't say this to you at the session I'm writing about, but I kind of see it as poetic justice that politicians' kids are going to perish and suffer alongside the rest of us. It's not fair on those kids of course, but then it's not fair on other kids either. They'll just have to curse their politician parents, just like we curse their politician parents. That's the only satisfaction we can hope for.

Our leaders are like kids anyway, truth to tell. Really immature. Doubtless they still suck their thumbs and take a bit of cloth to bed, something they can rub between their fingers for comfort. (My sister had one of those for years, a dirty grey piece of silk from the edge of her baby blanket.) They probably still wet their beds and all.

They act compulsively without thinking, and have tantrums if they don't get their own way. And they're totally narcissistic. How can they not be if they're happy to put their own interests and welfare above those of their own children? It's just me, me, me! *Why can't I have all the sweeties, mummy? Why do I have to share them with my friends?*

If it's true that all these presidents, prime ministers, dictators, kings, queens and leaders around the world are behaving like children (and it is true), it must follow that they shouldn't have children themselves. It's both criminal and insane – criminally insane – that they're allowed to reproduce. They should be sterilised the moment they're elected.

As soon as they assume office, it should immediately be explained to them – in very simple language – that they have extremely low IQs, are hopelessly immature and irredeemably selfish, and are therefore forbidden to reproduce while holding office. (If they already have children, then those unfortunates must be taken out of their *care* (ha ha ha), and placed in a foster home.)

Basically, they're the lowest of the low: selfish, short-sighted, more than happy to commit genocide if it means hanging onto their overly-generous pensions, and immensely and excessively stupid. If I explained to one of them in a quiet, friendly way, just how self-interested and myopic he or she was – you know, like I was addressing the family dog – they'd react in exactly the same way as the family dog: wag their tail and look at me adoringly. That's how much comprehension a politician would have of what I'm saying. It speaks volumes about the size of their brain.

They're like Louis XV – or was it the XVI? – the one who said: 'Après moi le deluge.' The shit will hit the fan after I'm gone, or words to that effect.

Basically, King Louis didn't give a toss about what happened after he died. Which is no different to the agreement-destroying, forest-flattening, coal-wielding, island-flooding, self-serving fools in charge of the world today, including our very own Prime Moron. The dangers of doing nothing must be as obvious to them as it is to the rest of humanity – unless, as well as having ant-sized brains, they're also blind, deaf and dumb. Which I suppose is a possibility.

Politicians are the maddest of the mad, no doubt about it, yet they're the ones who insist most vehemently that they're sane. But it's not possible to ignore global warming and at the same time declare yourself to be a sane member of society. A sane person would lack the imagination to act in such a mad, crazy, insane way. They couldn't do it.

Therefore, the odds are, there will be politicians locked up in here with me. There must be, seeing that every single one of them is fucking nuts.

You may understand from the above that I don't like politicians. And isn't that a sure sign of my sanity?

Hugh came to see me this afternoon. It's his second visit, yet no one in my family has come near the place since I got here, and it's been weeks. What do you make of that? Zoe hasn't even visited me, but then I suppose that's not so surprising, considering what happened.

The only reason my best friend is allowed in, he let slip on his first visit, is because my parents have given him permission. 'They think I'm a good influence on you,' he confided, and we both laughed. Hysterical.

It's always good to see Hugh. He never asks about what happened, which is a relief. We just don't go there. It's not like he avoids the subject, or treats it like some monstrous ear-flapping elephant in the room. That would be too obvious, and make us both feel uncomfortable. It's more like he doesn't think it's worth talking about, like it doesn't interest him at all. Which is how I feel. It's history.

I asked him, 'Do you think I'm like them?' and waved an arm vaguely to encompass the gathering of weirdos around us. These include the man who endlessly paces the perimeter of the living room (a *living* room full of the *lifeless*), head down, arms hanging loosely by his side. He does this for such long periods of time, I worry he'll create a crop circle in the carpet. Another man sits in an armchair and stares fixedly at every person in the room before giggling wildly, sometimes also pointing, as if he's spotted something each of those people is completely unaware of, like a bogey hanging out of his nose or his fly being open. Seriously uncool.

I was interested to hear Hugh's answer about whether or not I could be compared to these men of challenged sanity. I trusted him to tell the truth. He looked around the room. 'I can't see it,' he said, shaking his head. I considered this a bit non-committal coming from my best friend, and thought that was it until he added, 'When I think about it, I guess you're somewhat similar to Alastair.'

This particular patient is the disheveled individual who sits in his armchair by the window all day, jerking himself off. He must be excited by the bushes in the garden or something. Now and again one of the nurses will try and make him stop, but most of the time they leave him to it. You know, a bit like a parent will leave a child to play with his Gameboy for hours on end. At least he's keeping quiet and entertaining himself.

'I am, yes,' I said to Hugh. 'I can see that.'

Alastair carries out this so-called self-abuse beneath a blanket, which is a blessing for the rest of us, I guess. I wonder if he's happy tossing himself off all day. What's really freaky though, he never seems to come. So why bother? The fact I prefer to do that kind of thing in the privacy of my own bed, could that be further proof of my sanity?

Hugh grinned. 'Are you as compulsive?'

'I think so.'

He laughed (which he always does in a kind of apologetic way, his head lowered like he wants to stifle too great a display of happiness). 'I'm surprised you don't wear glasses in that case,' he said. I looked blank. 'Too much of that can make you go blind. Did no one ever tell you that?'

'Of course,' I lied. Neither of my parents would ever have told me something like that.

I think my admiration for Hugh stems from the

fact that he knows where he is in the world. Where he stands. I suppose I'm saying that he knows who he is. I've always been envious of such people, the fact they never seem to doubt. Dad's like that (but not mum). And my sister Sam's like that too, if not now then she certainly will be in a few years' time, when she's a bit older. The Prime Moron is definitely like that, rooted in his certainty, like an immovable 500-year-old tree. It doesn't seem to make any difference if they're good people like Hugh, or bad people like the PM, they have total faith in themselves.

I'm kind of sad I'm not like that too. I don't know where I stand in the world, or what I believe, or who I am. I kind of wander aimlessly, like I'm always trying to work out exactly where I am, and where the exits and entrances are around me.

Take climate change. You might not think so, but my beliefs are so tenuous, they're constantly in danger of being overwhelmed by the cacophony of the deniers who surround me. Although I can convince myself that my opinions are worthwhile and even correct, the certainty of the opposition quickly weakens me and makes me doubt. I despise myself for this, for allowing them to turn me into a St. Thomas.

Hugh's too strong to be overwhelmed, despite his modesty. That's maybe why I enjoy his company. I find it reassuring. Sometimes we speak a lot when he visits, both of us talking over the other, sometimes we sit in silence. We're comfortable with both.

Now and again one of the patients will approach him, tug at his sleeve to gain his attention, then shout in his face: 'Who are you?' He's very relaxed about it all – which is typical of Hugh.

'Have you noticed how everyone shouts in here?' I ask him.

'They're scared no one can hear them.'

That was pure Hugh: very pragmatic, but at the same time sort of philosophical. 'Like me,' I said. He looks puzzled. 'No one hears me.'

He nods. 'True enough, Al. That's because you don't shout. Still, I hear you.'

'Thank you for that.'

As on his first visit, we were sitting by ourselves, on the outer edge of the room. We were watching the others. It's always interesting. One of the patients, Bernard, came in through the French windows from the dazzling light of the courtyard. 'Shut the door,' someone shouted at him.

'Please,' corrected one of the nurses, but the patient who made the demand ignored this reprimand. Bernard paid no attention to him either. He sat down with me and Hugh. 'It's chilly out there,' he said slyly, looking downwards, addressing the empty space between us, as if there might be a fourth person present.

'It's global warming,' Hugh said, more to make conversation than anything else, at least that's how it struck me. 'It's almost cold enough to start a bushfire,' he added for good measure.

Bernard stared at him for a moment, as if not following him, then burst out laughing. He put his head back and laughed until tears were rolling down his cheeks. It was a manic laugh. A nurse, some distance away, looked across at us and frowned. I know they don't like excessive displays of emotion, and usually treat them as signs of impending trouble, often rushing to fetch the nearest syringe or pill. I shrugged, just for her benefit. I shrugged like Bernard's laughter had nothing to do with Hugh or myself, and we had no idea why he was laughing so fanatically.

He's laughing like a madman, I thought, and wanted to share this (sane) insight with my friend, but at the same time didn't want to be rude to Bernard, who I think is kind of cool in his own weird way. It took him a few minutes to calm down. He thumped the sides of his armchair when he'd finished laughing. 'That's good,' he said.

'What's so funny?' I asked.

'His goose is cooked! His goose is cooked!' he shouted, pointing at my friend.

'Yeah?'

'Global warming will cook his goose. He's right: he's a dead duck. All you kids are.' Turning to Hugh, he added: 'You're a funny man, even though I can see why you're in here.'

I was about to explain that Hugh was a visitor, when he gestured to me to say nothing, and asked: 'Why's that?'

'Blaming this heat on global warming, man. That's crazy stuff.'

Hugh nodded, unfazed by Bernard's logic – or lack of – and pleased that this stranger found him amusing. He obviously had no desire to tell him that he wasn't a patient, instead turning to me and smiling like that was our secret.

Sometimes, if it isn't too hot – and we've had some blisteringly hot days already this year, with records being broken (as they seem to be with every passing year) – Hugh and I hang out in the grounds. Unlike most parts of the State, the grass is a lush green. The old gardener has just finished mowing it, and is putting the ride-on away in the shed at the top of the garden.

They turn the sprinklers on every evening – with signs aimed at the street to stop passers-by complaining: TANK WATER IN USE. Hugh still objects. 'You shouldn't even use tank water during a drought – at least, not to water a lawn.'

We were sitting side-by-side on a bench, staring out across the garden, when I asked him, 'So you don't think I'm like that lot?' Indicating with a nod of my head the house behind us.

'Of course not. Why do you ask? Though I have to admit, it was a bit crazy doing what you did' (referring to *that* incident, the one that got me locked up in here in the first place).

'Yeah, I know. You did warn me.'

I'M SURE YOU'VE HEARD THIS FROM MY FATHER ALREADY, BUT I want to give you my side of the story. I imagine that's what this exercise book is all about anyway, to give you my side of the story, even though you'll probably never read it.

When I first had the idea after the schools' demo against climate change, I immediately approached Hugh. It was the march that first got me serious about climate change, and I was keen to do more. I wanted to carry out my plan with him, not anyone else. But when I explained what I had in mind, he totally freaked. 'That's criminal. You can't do that, Alan, you'll end up in prison.'

Yes, right! I should have expected that response from him. Even though he's my best friend, he's sort of conservative. He's a year older than me to start with, and he's certainly more thoughtful than me. Probably far more intelligent too – OK, definitely more intelligent!

'They're the criminals, all of them' was the only reply I could think of at the time. 'I'm just fighting like with like, bro. It's the only way to strike back at these people. Make them aware of how they're wrecking the environment.'

'What they're doing isn't exactly illegal, Al, though I admit it's verging on the immoral.'

'Making the planet uninhabitable has to be illegal – and if it isn't, it should be. It's both illegal and immoral. It's a crime – no argument about it!'

We did argue about my plan, but my heart wasn't in it. He'd made up his mind, I could see that, and I wasn't going to fight with him and risk our friendship.

I want to make it clear: Hugh was keeping it one hundred percent. He refused to have anything to do with my plan, and wasn't involved in any way. I didn't tell him I was going ahead even if I didn't have his support, and I certainly didn't mention that I intended to contact the very people who'd wanted to get involved in our school's demo against climate change.

'They're not schoolkids,' was how Hugh described them to me at the time. 'They call themselves "climate anarchists".' There was a degree of awe in his voice when he said this, like he was fascinated, but wary – not wanting to get too close. He decided it was safer not to allow them to take part in our climate demo for that reason. But I remembered him telling me where in the city they hung out. It had stayed in my head.

I tracked the activist group down, and became a member. They eyed me suspiciously to begin with, but it coincided with the time I began to feel passionately about the government's inaction on climate change, and I think my anger and commitment convinced them I was the real deal. I finally settled on Dougal, a Scot, to help me carry out my plan, perhaps for no other reason than that I liked his sense of humour. He was older than me by about three or four years.

I had a coffee with him after one of the group's meetings. I was risking a lot telling him my idea, but I couldn't see an alternative. I was certain he wouldn't go to the police or anything like that, but I was worried that he'd tell the others in the group, and from there things might get out of hand – as in be taken away from me.

Dougal was enthusiastic. 'It'll be a grand change from blocking the entrances to coalmines' was his first comment. He wanted to involve one other person – Matt – and I agreed. I think he was worried about me being so young, and wanted to have a friend onboard too, someone he knew. We all swore each other to secrecy.

It's obvious to me now that I should have listened to Hugh, rather than get carried away like I did. With hindsight, I can see how amateurish the whole operation was. We decided to go ahead with the plan in August, when my father was overseas. Dougal and Matt arranged the van and the *apparatus* through one of their contacts – another activist from what I understood. I didn't want to know the details.

I stressed to Dougal how important it was to have a smart new van. A beat-up old rust bucket with blacked-out windows would be a disaster, attracting unwanted attention to ourselves before we even started. I thought a new van might even be a problem, but couldn't see any option.

I WANT ZOE TO VISIT ME. DESPITE WHAT HAPPENED BETWEEN us, I want to see her. So I guess now's as good a time as ever to tell you about her, even though you haven't asked me to.

Zoe's fire! Her hair's red, and sometimes – like when she's lying down and her hair is spread like an arc around her head – it looks like a halo of flames shooting out in every direction. A modern Medusa, but without the snakes.

We met at the KIDS AGAINST CLIMATE CHANGE march. Hugh was the organiser at our school. You probably know the movement started in Sweden, with Greta Thunberg, who's even younger than us. From there it spread to the UK, the Continent, the US – just about everywhere. It's lit, and done so much good. Greta's a legend.

We aren't at the kind of school that looks on demonstrations favourably, so it was quite something for Hugh to put up his hand and say he wanted to be a part of this environmental movement. Throughout the school's 'long and illustrious history' (their words), it's probably never had to consider giving pupils permission to take part in a demo, especially for a cause that would be a real gross-out for most of the parents. They're the kind of people who leave a huge footprint as they go about their daily lives: driving Porsches, flying back and forth across the world (in either Business or First Class), living in enormous houses, and devouring vast quantities of meat. They're doubtless descendants of the fiddling Nero, who regard global warming as something for the lower orders to worry about. Exactly like my own mum and dad.

Both of Hugh's parents are psychiatrists (how fucked is that!) – oops, sorry Dr. C. Please don't take that personally. All I meant was, they're almost certainly more open-minded (read left wing) than my parents. I think my mum and dad's attitude towards the demo would be similar to the MP who said something along the lines of, 'Schoolchildren should know their place, which is in the classroom, studying. They can't be allowed to run around the streets demonstrating against something they know nothing about.'

Even the Prime Moron got in on the act, saying something about kids already being anxious (he must mean about whether they'd be taken to McDonald's at the weekend, or get an iPhone for their birthday, or be allowed to sleep over at their friend's house that evening), without having to worry about climate change as well. A little condescending, I thought, but it definitely helped me make up my mind not to mention the demonstration to my parents. I knew they'd object, and it wasn't worth the hassle.

Mr. Marshall, the school's headmaster, prides himself on being liberal-minded, so it wasn't that surprising when he gave permission for anyone who wished to attend the rally to do so. The majority of students put up their hands because they thought it would be more fun than staying in school studying differential equations or whatever. I only went along because Hugh was the organiser. OK, also because by then even I was beginning to question the Government's lack of action on climate change. I didn't quite share Hugh's passion on the subject, but then he's always been a far more committed person than me on just about everything.

He's a mine of information on global warming. Like telling me how the Government was subsidising coalmines with millions of dollars a year, as well as giving approval for new ones to open. He says they justify their actions with 'worn out' arguments about growing the economy and reducing unemployment. 'That's as far as their thinking goes,' he says – 'the economy. But it's our future they're talking about, Al, a future they've as good as given up on.'

TBH, the demo was a bit of a fizzer. We marched down the town's main street with other schools in the area, waved our handmade banners, and chanted endless slogans. Only a few shoppers paid any attention. (In the city, the demonstrations had much bigger turnouts, there was a lot of media coverage, and those taking part were attacked in the Media by teachers and right-wing politicians. Some were even arrested. Sadly, we missed out on all of that!)

It was the first time I came up against people's indifference. It's true some people gawped at us, as if to say, what's going on here? A few passengers rubber-necked out of passing buses, *Oh look, there's something happening outside the town hall.* And the couple of policemen I saw regarded us with dead eyes, as if they were totally over environment demonstrations. They'd likely have been happier if they could have lobbed canisters of tear gas at us, or charged us on horseback with raised batons.

But it wasn't a complete waste of time. I fell in love! It was unreal, totally unexpected.

Hugh was at the front of our group, organizing the chanting and setting the pace or whatever it was he believed he was in charge of. I was back in the body of the group – basically by myself, even though I was surrounded by lots of people. As I said before, I wasn't sure I should even be there, and kind of kept my head down. I think I was worried dad would hear about this.

Everyone was chanting, talking, laughing – you know, generally carrying on, when I became aware of one voice in particular, over on my right. And the voice seemed to be directed in my direction. I turned… and saw a vision. Yes, yes, I know, what a cliché, blah, blah, blah, but it was true.

She had brilliant red hair, right down past her shoulders, and flawless pale skin. For some strange reason I thought of a damsel from medieval times (although not one in any kind of distress as far as I could tell). The lady of a knight, yes, sincerely. She even wore a flowing, loose kind of dress, tied with some kind of girdle round the waist. She should have been on horseback – a white horse, maybe naked, but best not go there…

She was staring straight at me – which immediately made me blush – and yes, as she chanted some slogan or other ('Save the planet!' or, 'Climate action now!' or whatever), it was like she was directly addressing me, but taking the piss at the same time. She was grinning quite unashamedly and openly, and I thought, *She can't possibly be smiling at me.* I looked round to see who she was smiling at, but there was no one else looking at her. Which meant I should smile back, just in case, it's only good manners. I tried to, but it was beyond me! I think I managed a faint, sickly grin, like a dying man might bestow on those around his bedside, but that was all.

She was nodding her head like she was saying, *Yes, I'm talking to you, and I fancy you.* That has never happened to me before, ever, and I was kind of struck dumb. She was fly – far too beautiful for me. My cheeks were burning. It was crazy, I must have been scarlet. She looked unbelievable. Despite the obvious mutual attraction – and it was obvious – I was incapable of moving. I couldn't take a single step in her direction, although I just about managed to continue walking forwards with the crowd. I scarcely dared look at her, staring at the ground in front of me like I was hoping to find a $50 note, and only glancing quickly at her every few seconds.

I suspected her smile was becoming ironic, maybe mocking because of my inability to approach her. Or maybe she'd picked me for a non-believer, an imposter at the rally, and concluded that she despised me. That was it. She thought I was pathetic because I wouldn't talk to her. And why wouldn't I talk to her? Because I couldn't. She might just be a person – you know, human like me – and it might be considered quite normal to chat to a complete stranger in the street, even though we didn't know each other – but that's it! We didn't know each other! That was the problem, we hadn't been introduced. I needed to be introduced, I needed someone to say, 'Alan, this is so-and-so' and 'so-and-so, this is Alan.'

Ohmigod! She was weaving her way through the other marchers towards me. It was like a slow dance, a step left, a step right, twisting her body first in one direction, then the other. She must have given up on me doing anything so she was taking matters into her own hands. Could I pretend that I hadn't seen her, that I was completely unaware of her existence? I could then act surprised if she spoke to me – no, *when* she spoke to me, because I knew she was going to. But, no, that wasn't possible, I couldn't do that. I'd already smiled at her – in a pathetic, half-hearted kind of way, true, but I had smiled at her. So, I could hardly pretend I hadn't seen her.

'Hi.' She was right by my side. I sensed she was about to grab my hand or link arms with me, and this thought was quite terrifying. It might even cause me to pass out. I became aware of the girls she was marching with staring at us, laughing and nudging each other, like they were finding our situation incredibly amusing. 'Oh, ignore them,' the red-haired girl said, 'they're jealous.' (They're jealous that this goddess was speaking to me, is that what she meant? Unbelievable.) She turned and gave them a pretend dismissive toss of her head.

'Do you think there's still time for us to fall madly in love before the world ends?' (I took it that she was referring to global warming.) Her eyes were so intensely green, I found myself staring at them, hypnotized. Yes, I was sinking into their depths. She was biting her lower lip. It was a gesture, like saying, *perhaps I shouldn't have asked you that question, but to hell, I'm glad I did.*

'I'm already in love.'

OMG, how crazy was that. I actually said that to her, 'I'm already in love.' Can you believe it. So unlike me. It just came out, so suddenly it was ridiculous, like I couldn't help myself. That was my attempt at a witty reply to her question. Clever, huh? Whatever. She stared at me, then shook her head, as if to clear it. Then she laughed, in a kind of generous, forgiving way, like she'd already forgotten my ridiculous statement.

She was perfect, a vision. Everything passed in a blur. Somehow – and I have no idea how – when we parted, we'd exchanged phone numbers.

MUCH LATER, ON OUR WAY BACK TO SCHOOL, I SAID TO Hugh, 'I've met this crazy chick.'

He stopped dead, and just stared at me. 'You're in love, aren't you?' As perceptive as ever.

I shrugged. How can you answer a question like that? 'Maybe.' Even though he was the only person I could possibly tell, I found it hard to admit to such a thing.

He slapped me on the back. 'Tell me about it.' Which I did.

He was more amused than anything else, but in a nice way. As with everything else, he's way more sophisticated than me, which probably explains why he always has girls flocking round him. He claims they're just friends, but I think he's being modest.

It wasn't until the next morning that Hugh and I got around to discussing the demonstration (the morning after I'd spent the whole night dreaming of Zoe. On a white horse. Naked).

'To be honest, I was hoping for some riot police,' he said, 'some scuffles, perhaps a few arrests. And there wasn't a single TV News camera anywhere near us, not one.'

I was genuinely shocked, although I guessed he was maybe being sarcastic. I certainly had no idea he felt that way. 'It's good there wasn't any trouble, Hugh. TV coverage would have been good, but not violence. 'Haven't you lost the argument when you use violence? You're resorting to the tactics of the enemy.' I wasn't even convincing myself on this.

'We have to shake people up,' he said. 'They're too apathetic. We have to make them care about global warming, goad them into action.'

The school kids' demonstrations are continuing. The Scandinavian girl – Greta Thunberg – went to New York and gave a speech to the UN. Although she was very passionate and eloquent, and everyone applauded, a few cried, and she was given a bunch of flowers, I suspected it would eventually come to nothing. But that doesn't seem to be happening yet. Although the movement has definitely quietened down – with everyone trying to study, I guess – it's hasn't exactly fizzled out. But I can't help feeling our concerns about the climate will be swept under the carpet – as usual. We don't count obviously, and being ignored like that really bugs me. It's like everyone's turning their back on our future.

It was around that time that Hugh reminded me of the polling results before the last election. 'They showed that something like 80 per cent of the population were concerned about climate change and wanted whoever they voted for to do something about it. They then voted for a bunch of fascists who refuse to acknowledge that the rise in CO_2 emissions might be caused by us, and insist on continuing to mine coal for the sake of the economy. That's kind of crazy, don't you think?'

He always sees both sides of any argument – unlike me – and is always interested to hear the other person's point of view. Whereas I think those on the other side are stupid, blind, or ignorant. They make me mad (hahaha).

It's certainly not easy to give complete and utter idiots the benefit of the doubt when it comes to climate change and the likely extinction of our species. It's like lying beneath the blade of a guillotine and saying to the guy holding the lever, 'Well, yes, I can see where you're coming from.'

But I was more interested to talk to Hugh about Zoe. Again. We've texted each other endlessly. Now we've arranged to meet. I wanted my best friend's advice.

It goes without saying that dad was furious when he found out that our school had been allowed to attend the demonstration. 'You've stabbed me in the back' was how he put it. He made an appointment with Marshall, and tore strips off him, even threatened to withdraw me from the school. 'No child of mine's going to get caught up in such insanity. This climate change nonsense is nothing more than a media beat-up.' Mr. Marshall was too diplomatic to react.

THE FIRST TIME I SORT OF UNDERSTOOD WHAT DAD DID FOR A living, I was about eight, and me and mum and Sam were watching TV. We were staying with granny. I think dad was in the States on business when it happened, which would explain why he wasn't with us. (It was pretty unusual for him to be with us anyway, him being a workaholic and all.)

It didn't take long for me to work out that what we were watching on the screen was connected to him in some way, and I remember wishing that he was with us to explain what was going on because I didn't feel granny or mum were doing a very good job of it. I was too young to take in what was going on, and still at an age when dad was the GOAT, he could do no wrong. It was like I was thinking, 'This is daddy's work, this is what he does when he's not at home with us.'

It was exciting, awesome sight, I clearly remember that. Although it was on the News, it was only on screen for a minute or two, but I remember Sam channel-hopping all evening (and no one objecting) as she tried to find the same story on other stations. I'm not sure what she was hoping for, maybe that dad would be interviewed. We'd seen that often enough before, and it was always exciting to see him in a studio like some kind of rock star.

The flames were leaping into the night sky, but were almost obliterated by huge clouds of black, billowing smoke. The giant rig was surrounded by tugs spraying jets of water onto the inferno from every angle. They didn't seem to be having any effect – which was great as far as I was concerned. I didn't want the fire to go out. It was like some kind of private fireworks display, and I was wide-eyed.

I was sitting on the sofa between mum and granny. Sam was sitting in one of the armchairs. (The fact my mother was watching TV when she normally never watches TV was an extraordinary event in itself.) I remember her looking shocked, which I'd never seen before either, and knocking back the G&Ts, which I had seen before. She kept on saying, 'Oh my God,' but also, although slightly less often – almost as if she'd only just thought of it: 'Your poor father.'

I had absolutely no idea how dad was connected to

this spectacular display on TV, or why he was my 'poor father', but immediately supposed he must be on one of the tugs, maybe even on the rig itself. That thought was both terrifying and exciting. But whenever I turned my head to look up at mum and ask, 'Why?' she didn't answer. She simply patted my leg and said, 'Shh, not now, darling, I'll answer your questions later.' She never did.

Then – and I can't remember if this happened when we first saw the footage of the fire in the Bay of Mexico, or whether it was at another time, maybe the next day – the rig shrank into something that looked very twisted and black, like a nightmarish, structural Hunchback of Notre Dame. That was when the tugs pulled away from it, as if they'd decided to abandon it to its fate. They continued hosing it down, but now from a safer distance. They kept this up until the whole structure keeled over to one side, slowly and painfully like an old man, and the next minute (or that's how I recall it) it disappeared from sight. All that was left on our TV screen were the tugs and a flat expanse of empty sea.

This empty sea was making an enormous statement, like it was really full of significance. It was kind of emphasising what should have been there, but which we now could no longer see. It struck me that a magician had waved his wand and the vast oil rig – normally so unyielding on its massive steel legs – had sunk beneath the waves.

What we could also not see on our small TV screen at the time was the enormous, black oil spill spreading slowly in every direction, barely hindered by the containment barriers floating ineffectively on the surface.

None of us were talking. We simply stared at the screen, the virtually blank screen, as if we'd just witnessed a magic show and the magician himself had suddenly disappeared before our eyes, leaving a bare stage and a puzzled, dumbstruck audience.

'Sick!' Sam unhooked her legs from the armrests of her chair and straightened up, suddenly intent on other, more important matters – like her stomach. 'Mum, can I get something to eat?'

'What do you want, Samantha?'

'I don't know, I'm hungry that's all.'

Mum sighed. Granny interrupted her: 'Help yourself to whatever you can find in the fridge, darling.'

As Sam got up, I asked if I could get something too, and followed her out of the room – much to her annoyance. 'Copycat!'

I wanted to ask her if dad was all right, but all she would say was, 'Course, he is, knucklehead. Why wouldn't he be?'

I needn't have been concerned. Later, I found out he was in New York on business anyway – before the disaster even happened. He flew down to New Mexico immediately, but only in an advisory capacity, and he hadn't gone out on the Bay. He was never in any danger.

Nevertheless, he returned home a hero. I'm not sure if I picked this up from mum or Sam, or if it was simply my own interpretation, but it was like he'd grown in stature. He'd been overseas to fight a great battle, and had returned victorious.

We had a special meal, and my sister and I were allowed to stay up late. I remember dad opening a bottle of champagne, and giving me a sip. And that night, and over the following weeks, friends of my parents proposed toasts, gushed congratulations, and I remember one individual – a neighbour – slapping him on the back and saying, 'Great work, JC. Great work.'

(Everyone calls him JC – short for John Cunliffe– like they expect him to rise from the dead or something. For all I know, perhaps he's already performed that particular miracle. I certainly think he likes the abbreviation – like he deserves nothing less than to be named after the Son of God.)

There were endless retellings of the disaster – referred to by almost everyone as 'the incident'. (It was the first time I remember hearing a euphemism.) My father used expressions like, 'It was a close call,' and 'Not as bad as it could have been.' There was all this talk about the positives: 'We'll be back in production before long… It looks like we didn't lose too much oil… Managed to cap it pretty quickly, all things taken into account... Our PR boys have done a good job getting our side of the story across…'

I was as pleased to hear this news as everyone else, despite being about eight years old, and I don't remember any signs of guilt or criticism from anyone. (It wouldn't have surprised me at all if someone had told me that every single one of these friends or hangers-on was a shareholder.) Mind you, I didn't understand half of what was said, so I found my father's words both reassuring and comforting, and I totally believed everything he said. Truth is, I was so happy I grinned like a Cheshire cat – my dad was a hero.

Only when I was older did I find out that around 5,000 barrels a day spewed into the sea after the rig exploded, the oil slick was about 100 miles in diameter, and the well eventually had to be permanently capped. It was an environmental disaster. But I knew nothing about any of that at the time.

I also remember – despite paying little attention to it then – dismissive snippets from visitors to our house about bird and marine life being affected, like it just wasn't important. But their comments were at odds with what I saw on TV – shots of seagulls and pelicans covered in oil, and dead fish being held up close to the camera, mouths gaping, suffocated. Only to young people like myself must these tragic scenes have been unfamiliar.

I didn't like having this shoved in my face, finding it both upsetting and distasteful. I sensed – and this is a complete guess – that this story about the local flora and fauna was competing in some way with, and was maybe even critical of, my father's story. I came to really dislike the earnest and angry people who were speaking on television about the birds and the fishes. I could see that they were different, and my parents behaved towards them, or spoke about them as if they were the enemy.

They looked rough, these people (or *hippies* as dad called them), the men often with beards and wearing beanies and rubber boots, and the women in trousers and old jumpers or windjammers, their hair uncombed. They weren't like the oil company executives I was more familiar with. Nevertheless, I was reassured to hear my dad say, 'We have the country's top environmentalists on board, and they've reassured us that marine life won't be affected long term.'

I also remember him saying that some of the local fishermen ('Mexicans', said with just a hint of not wanting to spend too much time talking about them), 'are trying to make out that it's worse than it is, that their livelihoods have been affected. They're trying to take advantage of the situation to obtain a big payout, but our lawyers have assured us that we won't have any worries on that score. The locals are blowing everything out of proportion in order to claim compensation. It's a shame, because our company does so much for local communities wherever we work, as well as boosting the local economy. Doubtless it will come right in the end. As you know, we care deeply about the environment...'

I was totally persuaded. I never spoke, just listened, wide-eyed on the very edge of the circle of grown-ups. I even welcomed the news that 'Our share price has already recovered its earlier losses.' I was inordinately, innocently pleased at this news, even though I didn't understand it. But it sounded to me like a 'good thing'. I was carried along by my father's enthusiasm and reassuring words. He's a born salesman, always has been.

Looking back, I can see that it was all good news – at least that's what I heard. There was no bad news. Scarcely surprising, I suppose. Being so young, all I could see was that my dad had this incredibly glamorous and exciting job, even though it mostly involved sitting at a boardroom table rather than standing on a storm-tossed oil platform kilometres out to sea.

Being cocooned from the outside world as I was, I simply did not hear any negatives. Bad news happened a long way away, in a different world, so far away it never reached my ears – apart from the odd hint at social occasions like those I've just mentioned, occasions when any negative news was either downplayed or dismissed outright.

Apart from my age, I think my attitude was also affected by the simple fact that this was all about my dad. And being my dad, I loved him unconditionally. In my eyes, he could do no wrong.

I ADMIT TO FINDING IT DIFFICULT TO BELIEVE THAT YOU think I should be locked up, that any sane person, especially a psychiatrist, could think I was insane. Some kind of committee – pushed by my father's company – was doubtless briefed to declare me mad, to sign all the papers, and you now get paid a lot of money to go along with that decision. Good for you, I guess.

That lawyer friend of my dad's (can't remember his name) doubtless proposed the 'insanity defence'. I've heard him talk about it – usually rail against it. But I'm sure he would have seen it as absolutely ideal for his friend's son. 'Perfect for your boy, JC. It means he'll avoid a prison sentence, but get to cool his heels in a mental home for as long as is convenient for you.' Fair enough, I suppose – if you don't mind every Tom, Dick and Harry thinking you're mad.

What fascinates me right now is: do the other guests in the fading splendour of this granny-like home, think they're sane, like I think I'm sane? Or do they actually understand that they're mad?

(I've noticed that the staff here tend to refer to this place as either a 'home' or a 'facility'. They use the first when they're trying to reassure a patient – like literally make him feel at home – the second when they think the patient needs a cold dose of reality.)

Maybe you're taken in by all their rubbish, maybe you're not. Maybe you just go along with my father like everyone else. I can understand how that would make your life a good deal easier. He doesn't like to be opposed. And for all I know, he's a benefactor of this place, although I doubt mental health clinics are a cause he strongly believes in. 'Get over it!' would more likely be his attitude towards those with mental health issues. But I suspect it would be a good tax dodge putting your money into some kind of charitable cause like this, and that would definitely appeal to him.

Anyway, Dr. Craig, I certainly hope you're not placing me in the same category as the other losers in this place. Look at Mr. Colling for crying out loud.

He's standing immediately in front of me as I write this, and it's surely obvious to you – even to those outside the medical profession – why he's in here. Imagine pretending to be Napoleon on a day like this. It has to be forty degrees outside, and he's spent most of the day strutting round the room, sweat pouring off his fat, vacant face like a waterfall. He's wearing some kind of outdoors jacket, which must be unbearably hot, but I guess he's wearing it because it gives him somewhere to wedge his arm across his chest, like his idol. He stares at the floor, a deep frown on his face, as he struts back and forth. I wonder what he's thinking about. Maybe nothing, maybe his defeat at Waterloo, maybe what we'll be getting for dinner. Who knows.

I said to him the other day (I was only trying to humour the deluded soul, to be friendly), 'I studied you in history, you know.' He looked at me like I was a complete idiot, then turned his back on me. Crazy stuff. But at least I tried to speak to him, so it's not my fault. I even addressed him as 'L'empereur' – very different to moping Marcus, a belligerent manic depressive, who insists on calling Napoleon Mr. Colling, despite the man shouting at him so many times, 'I'm the Emperor! Napoleon bloody Bonaparte!'

It's the most common form of delusion of course, thinking you're Napoleon. Not sure where I heard that, probably from Hugh's parents. The sad thing is, Mr. Colling doesn't strike me as being an educated man. I mean he obviously went to school and stuff, but how much does he know about the man he's imitating? Not very much, I suspect – maybe only that he kept his arm strapped across his chest. How much more does he need to know? Mr. Colling's Napoleon probably lives in Tullamarine rather than the Tuileries, is married to Jazmin rather than Josephine, and battles with the postman rather than the Prussians. So why bother quibbling over the historical truth?

I wonder what Napoleon would make of this obsession, so many nutters thinking they're him. Would he be flattered, or would it drive him as mad as the people who imitate him? Crazy thought! Still, I only score Mr. Colling one out of ten for originality. I've got more time for him than Alastair, however.

Outside, in the courtyard where the patients smoke, the sun is blinding. It's so brilliant it bounces off the aluminium-framed chairs, and the upright of the umbrella like some kind of celestial pinball. It makes me hot just to look out there. I can make out a slither of blue sky at the top of the window, above the courtyard wall, and I watch an occasional bird fly past as it goes about its business. Each bird – every single one of them – looks beautiful, but maybe that's just because I'm locked up in here and they're free.

It's pretty obvious (at least to me) why these odd-balls have been put away. You don't need a lot of time to work it out. Which doesn't preclude *them* looking at *me* and thinking exactly the same thing. I can see that. Next time Hugh visits, I'll ask him what he thinks. Does he think *I'm* mad, or does he think *they're* mad? I'll ask him to tell me the truth.

As soon as my mind goes down this track, I begin to wonder if *he* could be mad. Could Hugh actually be the mad one, even though he's walking around in the outside world like he's a sane member of society (ha ha ha)? Like he's got all his marbles, but perhaps he's the one who's as nutty as a fruitcake?

What I'm saying is, it's all relative. Madness is a relative thing – yeah, all my *relatives* are definitely mad! It's in the eye of the beholder, or whatever the expression is. Hugh's fighting the war against global warming, therefore he must be mad. That's the so-called sane man's argument.

My proposition is that our world isn't run by politicians, but by lunatics and clowns intent on the destruction of everything we love. And their only comeback is to accuse *me* of being mad – which is either a sane or insane response, depending on your point of view.

Enough of that. (It does my head in.)

I first knew something was up was when a nurse suggested that Alastair might like to take a walk in the gardens. Seeing that everyone – patients, staff and visitors – always seem to accept him as part of the furniture,

I thought this was strange, especially when he invariably displays a marked reluctance to interrupt the goings-on beneath his blanket.

No sooner did Alastair – hand still firmly on todger – exit through the French windows with his minder, than Zoe burst into the room. Which explained everything. The staff obviously consider her far too young and innocent to witness Alastair's recreational pastimes. Ha!

She was smiling at everyone, and dispensing many cheerful hellos. I was so surprised to see her that I must have been open-mouthed, just like my fellow inmates. They averted their eyes and lowered their heads almost as if they found it too difficult to look at her. She did look incredibly beautiful, and I wondered briefly how she could have ended up as my girlfriend – if she was still my girlfriend.

She plonked herself down in a chair next to me, quite relaxed and at home, then thought to take my hand and kiss it. She was playing to the gallery, and I could see that everyone in the lounge was transfixed. Even I was grinning like an imbecile.

'You never told me your dad was an oil man.'

That's what she said straight off.

'Didn't I?'

She shook her head. 'Doesn't matter, Al, but it would have been nice if you'd told me what you were going to do.'

'I didn't want to involve you. Just in case.'

She laughed. 'Why not? I'd have supported you, you know that.'

She dropped the subject. I stared at her. I knew I was still in love, I felt it, even though I haven't seen her since – well, since that fiasco weeks ago.

She asked me about the other patients. She was looking round the room like someone visiting the Madame Tussaud's Chamber of Horrors, but also like she was amused by all the staring faces.

'Poor Al. You don't deserve this. You're not like them.'

'You don't think so? Well, thank you for that.'

What had gone before was never mentioned by either of us. I was grateful for that, and anyway, I've already forgiven her.

I don't want to tell you about that yet, Dr. Craig. It's too embarrassing. I may get round to it one day. I guess.

You keep asking me about my dad. If I'm honest (which I'm trying to be in this exercise book), I'm worried that if I don't say anything nice about him, then it will be used against me and you'll keep me in here even longer than you have already.

I find it hard to write about him, but I'll have a go nevertheless. I suspect you're asking me to keep this notebook simply to clarify my own thoughts, rather than because you want to read about him yourself. I've spoken to you about him often enough, in group therapy, but there's plenty more I can say – and I'm not talking about that dumb biography stuff: he was born in such-and-such a year, had three siblings, is now balding and middle-aged, and so on and so forth. That's boring.

If I went back to the beginning, how would I start?

I've always been a bit wary of him. I'm not sure why. It's not like he's ever hit me or anything. But he's not exactly approachable. He's more distant than anything else, but that's maybe because he gets so caught up in his work. I didn't see much of him when I was growing up, as he was always away on business.

If he wasn't in the office at the beginning of term, he would sometimes drive me to school. I don't know why he bothered – I didn't really want him to. He could be in a bit of a mood, like he couldn't spare the time and had more important things to do than drive me around. He spent most of the drive on the phone anyway. I preferred it if mum took me, but would have been happier still to go by train, like most of the other boarders.

What was weird was that he only drove Sam to school if she started on the same day as me, otherwise it was up to mum to drive her or to put her on a train. (I should explain: our schools are only a few kilometres apart.)

I was sent away to boarding school at the age of seven. My mother always made out that it was his decision, and that she didn't want me to go away so young. But she never argued with him about this. She admitted as much to me once. I wasn't really bothered to be honest. I felt I had some control over my life at school, un-like when I was at home – which is like the wrong way round, surely? At home, my parents, and even Saman-tha, were always telling me what to do, and that really got to me. I've always been like the least important per-son in the house.

Sam went to school a couple of years before me, and she didn't complain either. I don't think either of us could wait to get out of the house. Our schools were only an hour or so from the city, on the coast, so it wasn't a problem going home for the odd weekend if we felt in-clined – but it wasn't often that we felt inclined.

Sometimes people ask why we were sent off to school so young. I think it was because our parents were too caught up in their own lives to involve themselves with ours. Also, dad's from England where I understand it's kind of expected to send kids off to boarding school as soon as they're born. His argument was: 'It didn't do me any harm'. He actually used to say that to Sam and me. He used the word *harm*, and insisted school at that age would do us good, set us up for life. Yeah, right. Hahaha!

We rarely spoke when he drove me, although he sometimes chatted to Sam if she was with us. If he did speak to me, it was rarely about anything important. So, unless he was listening to Wagner, or someone equal-ly depressing, we sat in silence. It was like driving in a padded cell, the outside sound-deadened world – way,

way out there somewhere – a distant murmur. The cars we passed looked as if they were from an earlier age.

There was one occasion when I wanted to talk to him about climate change, but such conversations were never easy. He likes to keep to himself, even when he's with his own family. I wonder at times if he's lonely. Sometimes I'll interrupt his train of thought, and he actually grimaces, like it hurts him to reply.

(You'll doubtless make a note of this disclosure – if you read this one day – and diagnose my problem as Infantile Parental Deficiency or something. But how far is that going to get us?)

Sometimes he made an effort to speak to me, but it was somehow obvious that it was an effort. It's like he was a learner driver, concentrating really hard, trying not to make a mistake.

This…is…how…I…must…speak…if…I…am…to… make…conversation…with… Alan… Like a robot, that's how he often spoke to me. Like his programming was still very rudimentary.

He would ask meaningless questions about how my studies were going. I'm convinced this was because he's concerned that he's made a bad investment sending me to this particular school. He asked Sam the same questions if she was with us, but she was just rude to him, or she'd argue with him. I think that's why she's his favourite, being the only one in the family who doesn't accept everything he says. She stands up to him. But it's easy for daughters to get away with stuff like that with their fathers, I've noticed that before, with my friends' dads.

Now and again, he pretends to take an interest in what he thinks are my interests, like cricket – which isn't really an interest of mine anyway, certainly not super special. But his efforts are too blatant, and it's all too painful, so it soon comes to an end. Like he's driven into a dead-end street, and finds that he then has to reverse out.

On that occasion I'm telling you about, when I wanted to talk about climate change, I think it was the last time he drove me to school. I made the basic error of breaking the silence, which was stupid because it was kind of peaceful in the car (until I broke it). I'm not sure why I bothered. Perhaps because Sam wasn't with us. Anyway, it was a mistake.

You have to understand – and I'm sure you do by now – that although dad and I live in the same house, we're virtually strangers. It's either because he's always distracted, or he finds me boring. Or immature. Or simply not worth talking to. I don't know.

We have very different views on most things. I'm not really sure he loves me, although he probably does, but I certainly kind of love him. It may just be admiration, of course, on my part.

He was overseas for most of my childhood, or that's how I remember it. He was like a visitor to the family home, not like someone who lived there with us. He flew first class. I knew that because, when I was small, he always brought his toiletry bag home for me. I loved all that stuff – the moisturisers, lip balms, bed socks, eye masks and ear plugs, the miniature toothbrushes and toothpaste, and the cologne. This 'gift' didn't cost him anything of course – neither money, nor time – but of course I didn't know any better.

As he went higher up the company, he flew by company jet. I was older then, and this impressed me, especially when mum, Sam and I went overseas with him, on holiday once. Now he's head of the company, he has his own plane, and doesn't have to share it with anyone – not even us it appears. Which means there are no more toiletry bags. I suppose I'm now too old for handouts anyway.

When I was at school, I sometimes didn't even realise he was overseas until I received a postcard from the Gulf, or Texas, or somewhere in South America or Europe. Perhaps I was being overly suspicious, but it invariably struck me that the postcard was bought for him by a secretary and posted for him by a secretary, with just a half dozen words or so written by him (or a secretary skilled in forgery). 'Dear Alan, you would like the architecture here. Dad.' With a photograph of the Jumeirah Beach Hotel or Burj Al Arab or similar on the front. That was it.

It often took me a whole morning to read one of his long postcards, catching up on all the exciting minutiae of my father's life. LOL.

But back to that particular drive to school. I think

it must have been pretty soon after the schools' demo against climate change.

I don't know why I did it. Maybe because there was more and more talk about global warming – in the Media, but also at school and among my friends. Everyone was beginning to ask questions and demand answers, and for the first time I was becoming genuinely concerned about what dad did for a living (mainly thanks to Hugh). Also, I was at an age when one begins to question the values of one's family, and to appreciate the amazing fact that there are people, outsiders, who think and do things completely differently to one's own family, to what one has been brought up to believe is the norm. But it still took courage to ask the question.

'Are you a climate change denier, dad?'

He was so surprised, he almost drove off the road. He recovered quickly however, and answered my question politely enough. 'I'm a sceptic, if anything, Alan. And you?' Turning the question straight back at me.

'I don't know. I'm not really sure.' I was a little lacking in courage!

He was listening to opera on the radio, although I couldn't tell you which aria or whatever. He turned it down, which alarmed me, like he was now going to give me his full attention. Then he said something about there having been changes in the world's climate for as long as the experts can go back.

'Do you know they can study rock formations that clearly show there have been periods of drought, floods and freezing temperatures lasting millions of years? This was way before Man set foot on the Earth, and way before our own carbon emissions. Those experts say that what we're experiencing now is no different to what our planet has already experienced many times before.'

He turned and smiled at me. This wasn't a common occurrence, so I remember it clearly. Maybe he felt it wouldn't be hard to defend himself against me. I was just pleased that I'd been able to summon up enough courage to speak to him, to question – no matter how vaguely – his profession. Unfortunately, his generous – or at least unaggressive – response convinced me that I should risk asking him another question. Just like we were two friends having an ordinary conversation, and now it was my turn to speak! My bad.

I was trying to keep it to that, to an ordinary conversation. I always avoid having an argument with my father because I worry that he'll get upset, but also because he has an answer for everything (often delivered in a slightly condescending way, like I'm an idiot). He can get quite defensive about his business at times – which surprises me. It's like he's aware – he must be! – of all the bad publicity about oil, coal and gas, and maybe it's beginning to get to him. He must know he's vulnerable, though I'm sure he doesn't expect to be attacked by his own family.

When I became a teenager, I think he lived in daily expectation of being prosecuted by me, like he'd given birth to some kind of nightmarish left-wing mutant. He doesn't feel that way about Samantha, I'm sure of that, quite probably because she has no idea what left- or right-wing actually means. Anyway, she's conservative, straight up.

My grandfather, on my mother's side, who always smelt of cigars and brandy, once said to me, 'Alan, everyone should be a socialist before they're thirty, and no one should be a socialist after they're thirty.' That has always kind of stuck in my mind, although I doubt it's a philosophy my dad would go along with. He'd believe no one should ever be a socialist.

I said to him (during this car journey), in what I hope was an easy-going kind of way, 'Your company isn't involved in fracking, is it, dad?'

He momentarily took his eyes off the road in order to stare at me. He was suspicious, I could see that, like he thought I might be about to openly attack him. 'In the States we are. Why?'

'Oh, I've just been reading about it.' It didn't come out quite as casually as I wanted.

'And what did you learn?'

'There were stories about fracking causing the water that comes out of household taps to ignite. I even read that it's been known to cause explosions.' I wasn't very coherent.

'If some of the chemicals leak into the water supply during the fracking process, it can cause problems, but it's rare. And the problem is always fixed, and compensation paid.'

It sounded like the official company reply. *Don't worry, folks, there's nothing to see here. Move along, please.*

'But from what I understand, it can affect the groundwater –'

He interrupted me quite abruptly. 'No, it doesn't.'

I pushed on: 'And can also pollute the air.'

The luxurious cocoon of the car suddenly felt claustrophobic and uncomfortable, and the ensuing silence weighed heavily on me.

'That's not right,' he said finally, almost like he could scarcely be bothered to utter the words. I wondered if that was it. I kept gazing stubbornly out of the car window. We were passing a 4-wheel drive, and a young kid in the back seat was waving a lollipop at me, the area all round his mouth a bright red, like a clown. He looked funny.

When dad spoke again, it sounded like he was doing his best not to be angry, like he was suppressing his instinct to shout at me or bang his hands on the steering wheel. 'Problems with fracking are rare.' He paused, possibly waiting for me to turn around. He almost sounded contrite, as if he was about to make a concession. I turned to face him.

He glanced in my direction. 'Problems only arise if it's not done correctly.' Then he turned quickly away, as if challenging me to continue the conversation. 'The advantages of fracking far outweigh any possible disadvantages.'

Yeah, right.

I wondered how he could say that. It contradicted everything I'd read. A minute later, he added: 'Fracking recovers shale oil and gas in such large quantities, it significantly drives down energy prices – to the extent that many oil companies don't make any money at all. And you might like to know –' (said as if people like me were some kind of ignorant, sub-human species) 'that by replacing coal, the practice has substantially lowered air pollution levels.'

The odd thing was, before he said that I was prepared to back down, like I normally do, and keep my thoughts to myself, but that final comment, stacking the odds in favour of oil, stirred me up in some way. It was so blatant, it goaded me into replying.

'That's not what I read on the Web.'

'You can't trust everything you read on the Web, Alan. Don't they teach you anything at that school? About fake news?'

I ignored that. 'Everyone says fracking uses enormous amounts of water – which often has to be transported long distances to the site.' He grunted. Was he agreeing, or disagreeing? 'And the groundwater's often contaminated with chemicals, many of which cause cancer. Also, the environmental costs are kind of mind-blowing from what I understand.'

I think, in hindsight, that my voice must have gone up a notch with each accusation I uttered. I hope not, but maybe.

The next thing I knew, he turned off the freeway and

we were driving through this small town that's about half way between the city and my school. It's like in the middle of nowhere. Dead.

I didn't realise what he was doing until he drew up at the front of the train station. 'Get your luggage out of the boot.' I hesitated, unsure what was going on, and unwilling to accept what I suspected.

'Do as I say,' he added quietly, 'now!'

Once I'd struggled to lift my two heavy bags onto the pavement and closed the boot, he shouted through the open passenger window: 'I'd remind you that all the privileges you enjoy, young man, are thanks to oil. Don't you ever forget that.'

And without another word, he drove off – if not for traction control, it would have been with a squeal of tyres.

I wondered if I'd won my first argument with my father. It would have been compensation enough for arriving at school almost three hours late.

I'm lying on my bed in my tiny room. It's about as interesting as the inside of a cardboard box. Apart from the single bed, there's a tall grey locker, a small table and chair, and a wastepaper basket. I'm trying to work out how this particular truth dawned on me, how the revelation came about.

Hugh was the one who asked me that all-important

question, the answer to which – let's face it – eventually led to me ending up in here, in the nuthouse.

I'm not sure why – and I appreciate this probably sounds a bit crazy (which is kind of appropriate, what with me being in here and all) – but I imagine it's like being the child of the owner of a high-class bordello. Really! Think about it.

When you're young, you probably consider your life to be quite normal: the many ladies wandering around all day in negligees, the corridor of sumptuously decorated bedrooms, the kind gentlemen visitors who feed you with sweets, and the half-naked women who sit you on their laps and laugh prettily as they tell jokes about you being such a ladies' man.

But as the years pass, as you grow older, there would be the slow revealing of the truth. It would arise from the accumulation of several incidents brought about by an offhand or innocent remark or two. It could be a comment by an older boy at school: 'What, your home is at number 54! For real, you live there?' Perhaps a sly wink from the postman and a 'How are all your girlfriends, young man?' Or maybe a playful remark by one of the gentlemen callers: 'What's a nice young man like you doing in a place like this?'

The point is, it would be cumulative, every comment and each incident building on its predecessor, until finally the curtains would part before your eyes: your mother is a Madame, she runs a brothel, a place where men and women fuck. How could I have not known for so long?

And I think it's been a bit like that for me with climate change. Little asides, small incidents, a gradual unveiling over many, many years, until that final question from Hugh, and my eventual appreciation of the truth.

'How do you feel about that, Al?' That's what he asked me.

He sounded like you, Dr. Craig. That's what you're always saying to people in our discussion groups – how does that make you feel? Hugh must have got it off his psychiatrist parents, I guess.

I didn't understand him at first. Why was it up to me to feel anything? Because that's what he was saying – not in a nasty way, he's never been like that – but matter-of-factly, as if he was simply acknowledging something that was obvious to both of us. He was interested to hear my side of the story. *Hey, this is to do with you, Al, so how do you feel about it?*

He genuinely wanted to hear my answer to that question. 'How do you feel about that, bro?' It must have been after yet another disaster, an oil spill on some pristine beach somewhere – I can't remember exactly what. Dad may have flown out to take charge of the situation – damage control, I think they call it. You know, hose down the bad PR, throw money at the local government, keep the media away, and bribe some official or other to say nice things about the company and their relationship with the local community.

I remember staring at my friend blankly. Perhaps I was trying to fathom his thought process. How did I feel about my father being in oil? I can't remember how I answered him, the exact words I used, because no one had ever asked me that question before. I really didn't have an answer, that's what it amounted to. I suppose I expressed regret, or said how unfortunate it was for the environment, or –. I don't know, I really don't know. Perhaps I expressed the hope that my father's company would be able to clear up the mess. Yes, it's possible I tried to excuse my dad.

(Those were probably still the days when I could have applied for the job of company spokesman, I was so blind to the truth. Those days are long gone.)

Hugh's question certainly made me think, perhaps for the first time. It can't just have been his question. More likely it was the cumulative effect of all those little incidents and comments I mentioned earlier. The way they built up over the years – perhaps from as early as the Bay of Mexico disaster – filling my mind with their toxic overload, right up until the moment he asked that seemingly innocent question: 'How do you feel about that, Al – about your dad's job?'

The real answer, which I didn't arrive at until weeks, or even months, later, was summed up in one word: shock. But other words, too: dismay, shame, maybe even embarrassment.

I started to read every article I could lay my hands on. I studied historical disasters (and there were plenty of those). I visited the reference section in the main library. I surfed the Net for hours on end. I looked at hundreds of photographs on Instagram. I poured over photographs of seabirds coated in oil, stranded on blackened beaches alongside dead fish. I read material from alternative sources – like the Greens and environmental activists, those who were fighting against the status quo. Normally, I never looked at that stuff, but I did now.

I also went back to my best friend. I asked him many questions. Hugh knew so much, and thought over issues much more deeply than me. I trusted him, respected his mind – far more than my own. What pleased me about his reaction was his quiet, reasonable response. He wasn't jubilant about winning some kind of argument over me. If anything, he was laid back – even more so than usual – not in the least blameworthy. There was no hint of him having won over the enemy (I'm the enemy because I'm my father's son), just a rational explanation of what was happening in the world – or *to* the world – and a foretelling of what the consequences would be for all of us.

Suddenly, I appreciated that this environmental catastrophe has been going on for decades and, more devastatingly, that my family has played an important part in it.

I'm not sure if my parents are Baby Boomers or Gen X. But it's like everyone says: their generation have totally, utterly and irredeemably stuffed up the world. They've raped it, tortured it, mutilated it, bled it dry, dragged it through the mud, burnt it at the stake, mocked and humiliated it. And that's just for starters!

Apart from the odd exception, they have never ever – *never ever* – cared for it in any way whatsoever. (It's like the world has been occupied for decades by bad renters, not proud owners.) And now, finally, just before they themselves die, they're watching our planet go through its death throes. They're as intent on killing it off today as they were yesterday, because they know there's not going to be any tomorrow. They're determined to leave their children with little more than a carcass.

It's a world that reminds me of the cheap plastic globe I had as a kid, the one I accidentally punctured with a compass.

Welcome to my father's life. My dad, the oil man. He didn't exactly hide what he did from me, he simply didn't talk about it. Or maybe he did, and I never listened.

I'll tell you what I don't understand. I try very hard to understand it, but it's obviously beyond me…

Of all the scientists in the world, who are generally-speaking, very, very clever people – they're certainly not idiots – and only interested in objective, provable facts (otherwise known as the truth), something like ninety-nine point nine per cent of those scientists say that humans are responsible for climate change. (Even Stinky Stevens, who teaches us Chemistry, says that.)

Every single one of them says that we are doing this to ourselves.

This body of scientists (probably even Stinky Stevens) doesn't have a vested interest in the results of their research, yet produces enormous quantities of data, scientific studies, charts, formulas and historical evidence to back their case. And having completed their decades of painstaking study in laboratories and out in the field, it's not like they've fronted up to the public with any degree of uncertainty. They're not saying, 'We think… We believe… It's possible… Maybe this or maybe that…'

There's no hesitation on their part. I only wish there was. But no, they present their findings using words like, 'This is definite… Climate change is now all but irreversible… If we do not act today, now, immediately, we are absolutely, certainly doomed… Mankind has caused this, and only mankind can put it right…'

That's how ninety-nine point nine per cent of scientists put it. The other point one per cent is employed by fossil fuel companies. Yet this tiny vociferous minority, like an annoying, barely discernible whine on the other side of the mosquito netting, still has its followers. And those followers, those fellow deniers, many of whom are unfortunately in charge of countries, either refuse to listen to the experts or refuse to believe them. They're sharp.

They say to those ninety-nine out of one hundred scientists: 'You're wrong. Global warming has nothing to do with Homo Sapiens'. (Haha haha, that gets me every time: sapiens, *wise!?* Yeah, right).

'Climate change is natural. It is part of a cycle that has happened many times before, throughout history, even before Man appeared on the earth. Stop worrying. Continue to burn coal – *clean* coal, if you insist. Continue to drive your super powerful, gas-guzzling, exhaust-belching cars. Continue to build old-fashioned power stations. Continue to consume like there's no tomorrow. Everything's fine! Everything's A-OK.'

It's like an ill person having an appointment with a doctor, who tells them that they're suffering from a terminal condition, and that they should take these little red pills if they want to give themselves the *chance* of a few more years. And the patient replies, 'I'm not going to listen to your expert opinion, doctor. I've decided to take these little yellow pills instead, and carry on living as I've always done.'

How can these people spout such nonsensical garbage? How can they continue to ignore the enormous body of scientific evidence? How can they be that stupid? Duh! If they were all politicians, I'd understand it. We don't expect *them* to grasp anything about what's going on in the world. But this minority of non-believers are supposedly intelligent.

Sure, some of them work for, or own, right leaning media outlets (like that megalomaniac nonagenarian), others are rich and run international businesses. They're doing all right, thank you very much, their profits usually earned from their cavalier treatment of both people and our planet. They want to maintain the status quo, no matter what the cost, maybe even swing things a little more in their own favour. If that's possible.

As for those ninety-nine out of one hundred scientists, there's no prevarication in their statements, no ambivalence, no ifs, buts or maybes. From what I can discover, their pronouncements a decade or two ago (before I was born) were less confident than what they're saying today. Today, they're like passengers in a car who can clearly see the oncoming truck on the wrong side of the road, and they're screaming at the driver of their car (a politician who bears a remarkable resemblance to my fellow inmate, the *wanker* Alastair) to get out of the way. *Now.*

These scientists remind me of the old black and white photographs I've seen – perhaps from the 1950s or 1960s – of men carrying sandwich boards with the message, THE END OF THE WORLD IS NIGH. The only difference is that the scientists of today are saying, the end of the world is right here, right now. They don't *believe* it's nigh, that it will happen, they *know* it's already happening. And if we don't change our ways, we're finished.

I find it hard to know how to react because I'm stunned.

I find it difficult to know what to say because I'm speechless.

I find it impossible to know what to do because I sense it's already too late.

I keep thinking of those crazy people who go over Niagara Falls in barrels. This is how they must feel. Spinning and bobbing wildly as they're swept towards the very lip of the Falls...

The interesting thing (according to Google) is that most of those insane dudes in their barrels die. I guess that's why none of them are locked up in here with me, even though they're obviously 100 per cent certifiable.

But the all-important question is, why do so many people ignore these scientists? The answer to that is easy – lobbyists. More and more, the global warming battle can be seen as one between scientists and lobbyists. One represents the objective truth, the other subjective vested interests.

Lobbyists are the lowest of the low, period.

They're soul-sellers who flog angles and opinions they probably don't even agree with. They promote anything toxic – cigarettes, coal, oil, nuclear power, foreign invasions – so long as they're paid truckloads of money.

Which they are, paid by the dirtiest and most harmful companies in the world. They're paid to persuade politicians and government ministers to back their employers' agendas, and they will cajole, bribe and bully to get their mankind-wrecking ways. They basically run the country.

But that's maybe underestimating our rulers, who –

it is just possible – are really clever, not the dunderheads we think they are. Maybe they have IQs that are off the chart, and simply use lobbyists to acquire more power and riches for themselves.

Today's political manifesto (with apologies to President Kennedy) is: ask not what you can do for your country, ask what you can do for yourself and your party. Bugger the country and the people.

When you tread the corridors of power, you have the chance to become seriously rich. Not rich like my dad, but rich like Bezos or Gates or Jobs (may he rest in peace in his solid gold coffin). That's what our leaders aspire to, to become billionaires. It's easy enough to do once you acquire power. Just ditch your conscience.

The lobbyists queue up at your door. Coal companies, power companies, agricultural businesses – all the people who enjoy fucking up the planet will knock on your door and beg you, with buckets of cash, to help them fuck it up some more.

'Mr. President, Mr. Prime Minister, Mr. Suharto (reckoned to be the most corrupt politician ever – wow, a distinction in corruption!), if you can see your way to passing this Bill, I'm sure we can see our way to helping you win the next election. Or we can put a few million dollars into your campaign coffers. Or we can buy a splendid home on the coast for you and your family. Or one for each of your ten children should you so desire.'

That's how easy it is. Our so-called leaders simply have to rubber stamp the demands of the lobbyists, and take their percentage. Everyone's happy (and rich), and the rest of us can go to hell in a handbasket, or whatever the expression is.

Greed is the root cause of everything, according to Hugh. It explains why our politicians do nothing about global warming. Why they won't even agree to discuss the problem with each other, and won't consider any solution, no matter how sensible it is, if it's been put forward by another party.

They're more interested in staying in power, in making money for themselves and their cronies rather than worrying about the country, about the ordinary people they're supposed to be looking after – including their own children and grandchildren.

You never ask to read what I write in my school exercise book, even though you were the one to suggest I put my feelings down on paper. You're either being discrete, or you're not interested.

Maybe you think my thoughts will be boring. It doesn't bother me if you do. It's probably just some weird form of therapy anyway, writing about yourself.

Don't think I mind doing it by the way, at times I almost enjoy it, and it certainly helps pass the time – which I have far too much of.

I've been thinking about dad's parting shot that time

he dumped me at the train station, about all the privileges I enjoy being thanks to oil. His comment was a good one – a bull's-eye.

I'm not sure how old I was when I first understood how successful he was. I mean, I saw our luxurious lifestyle clearly enough – the big house, flash car, the right suburb, the private school education, and the holidays-abroad – but it never struck me as being that different from anyone else's. It was like I thought our family was normal. Ha ha ha.

It's weird, but I remember being aware of our car, like super-conscious of it. I knew it was way better than almost anything else on the road, and it won me a lot of kudos at school. But I still found it embarrassing to stand out like that, to be so *obvious*, and I was more than happy to be able to hide behind its tinted windows.

So I guess this means I must have been aware, at least subconsciously, of being different to some people – the *real* people I viewed through those tinted windows, walking along the pavements: the mothers laden down with plastic shopping bags and crying babies, the men hanging round the front of bookies smoking cigarettes, the ordinary folk waiting at tram stops or eating their sandwiches on benches outside the shopping mall. I just didn't appreciate how different we were.

It never entered my head to question how dad paid for all of this. It wasn't a question I ever asked myself. Like most kids, I imagine. Even when I eventually came to appreciate that he worked for one of the world's biggest oil companies, I didn't join the dots – 'Ah, that explains why I enjoy such a lavish lifestyle!'

Incredible as it may sound, I didn't make the logical connection between big house, flash car, private school, lavish holidays and my dad's work. Yes absolutely, I was naïve. Or maybe just dense.

Eventually – and only three or four years ago, I suspect – I twigged: my dad was an oil man. That's when I *really* understood what he did. Oil paid for all of the good things in my life. Black gold was the source of the family's wealth.

Straight off I saw this as good news. It was like winning at Monopoly: I won, everyone else playing the game lost. But it wasn't like it was a calamity, or the end of the world. It was just a game after all, and that's how it was for me. I just happened to be on the winning side of a board game – the board game of life.

Swaddled in splendid isolation behind the locked gates of our mansion, with its swimming pool, tennis court and god knows how many bedrooms, I was drip-fed on good news. Everything I was told about oil was positive. Of course it was.

Dad, with the blind enthusiasm of a disciple, 'sold' me on the product he devoted his life to. I'm not sure this was intentional. It was more like he was so sold on the merits of oil himself, he took it for granted that his family was always right there behind him, being both supportive and appreciative. And, until recently, I was.

For as long as I can remember, dad explained to me

– not so much to Samantha – how oil kept the wheels of industry turning, and how this happened throughout the *civilised* world. (That 'civilised' was important: he considers a country that doesn't use much oil to be primitive.)

Oil was the source of our nation's wealth, the saviour of the Western world. It meant cars could run on the roads, planes could fly in the sky, and trains crisscross every continent. It made possible the generation of heating and electricity, and the production of asphalt and lubricants.

Best of all, oil meant we could enjoy those game-changing wonders of the modern world: plastics, synthetics and chemicals. (I can remember a time when dad praised the fact that plastic never broke down, or not for thousands of years. 'Plastic lasts forever, Alan,' he told me, like that was some kind of desirable miracle. But I haven't heard him say that for a while now.)

According to him, without oil, we would all be living in caves.

My recollections at school were a little different. They taught us that coal, steam power and iron production were the original catalysts of the modern age. Maybe dad sent me to the wrong school! He certainly wouldn't have been happy to learn that he was paying so much money for his son to be taught such disinformation.

He was forever enthusing about his product, always *gushing* (like an oil well blowout). 'How can we live without it, Alan? Look at America,' he once told me, when I was young and gullible, in his unbelievable-but-true voice: 'they consume an astronomical 20 million barrels a day. A day! Think how much that's worth. Think of the profit in that.'

Yes, that many barrels in a day, and an unnamed profit figure, but one with lots and lots of zeroes at the end. I was almost as awestruck as dad.

Of course, there were some things about oil he never told me. He didn't mention the huge amounts of carbon dioxide released into the atmosphere when oil is burnt. Or the environmental disasters caused by oil spills. Or oil's enormous contribution to greenhouse gas emissions (trumped only by coal). Or the damage to our eco-systems. No, I never heard him utter a word about any of that.

If he had a concern about oil, it was a fairly muted one: oil was a finite resource. One day it would run out. A few years back, many people thought like that. The demand was so enormous, the wells would eventually run dry. And at that point the party would inevitably end. (But only after his company had made trillions in profit, of course.)

TBH, such an outcome is unlikely to have been given much consideration by dad. It's a scenario, or finale, he could scarcely have allowed himself to contemplate. As likely as not, he prayed that this catastrophe would occur only after he died.

You asked me what my father's company did the

first time I saw you, even though you must have known. I remember answering straightforwardly enough. But if you asked me now, I'd probably give a different answer – perhaps just a two-word answer: rape and exploit.

His company rapes the environment. It drills huge holes in virgin forests and icefields, also at the bottom of oceans. Groundwater is contaminated. Rivers and lakes are polluted, forests bulldozed, wildlife killed. I could go on, but you probably think it's boring. Anyway, I'm sure you know it all already.

His company also exploits. Employees, the people who live near their oilfields, the general public. Everyone. The whole world and his dog. The only people who escape this exploitation – apart from the corroding of their consciences – are his company's shareholders.

Of course, his company's no different to any other oil company: it worships at the altar of Capitalism. Everything is done in the name of profit. Profit means growth, which means greater returns for shareholders, which means more profits for the privileged few… And so it goes, until the music stops.

And the music will stop. Either the oil wells will run dry, or the world's population will be incapable of inhaling sufficient oxygen to stay alive.

No wonder I did what I did. In the face of such immense destruction, I had to do something. In my opinion, I behaved with enormous restraint.

THEY PICKED ME UP ON THE EDGE OF THE CITY'S MAIN PARK, where the playground is, about a kilometre from our destination. Dougal was driving. He was wearing a suit and tie, and his hair was neatly combed back into a ponytail. He looked totally different (as in respectable). I was impressed – ok, maybe just surprised. Matt was in the back, sitting on the floor. He was dressed more casually, but still passably smart. It was getting close to six o'clock when I jumped in beside him.

When we reached the central business district, Dougal slipped discrete, readymade covers over our number plates. At the entrance to the underground car park, he lowered the driver's window to insert the pass card (the spare one I'd stolen from dad's study) into the machine. I closed my eyes, and prayed. What if it didn't work? How humiliating that would be in front of my newfound friends. We all held our breath... Suddenly the steel gates slid silently open.

'It's on the first level,' I whispered as we drove down the ramp. 'Head to the right... That far wall over there. Park just past that DIRECTORS ONLY sign.' He turned off the ignition. There wasn't a sound. I think we were expecting someone to appear out of nowhere, walk over to our van and demand to know what the hell we were doing. Rather than get out of the van, Dougal climbed over the seat to get into the back, and I climbed over into the driver's seat. If anyone approached the van, I was to say that I was dropping something off for my father – even though he was overseas, even though I was too young to have a driving licence (although they weren't likely to know that).

We waited, and waited, and waited. The three of us scarcely breathed. The minutes ticked by, but no one came near us. For almost three hours, we didn't move, and barely spoke. Matt fell asleep, but my mind was going around in circles, so fast I couldn't relax.

Most of all, I remember being kind of proud that I was doing something – however modest – to try and avoid the coming climate catastrophe. I was doing my bit. I was the proverbial man in the street, but I was still taking action. It was like I've always said: it's impossible to do nothing, even though that's what the government is doing. Me, I was past talking. No longer would I resign myself to turning off air conditioners and lights, recycling the garbage, and not eating meat. Those kinds of actions were little more than a drop in the ocean. I had to do more than that if I wanted to make a difference. And now I was.

It struck me (long before I was declared insane) that democracy excludes rather than includes. At election times, politicians pretend to listen and be interested in your concerns, but once they achieve their ambition and get into government, you don't see them for dust. Until the next election of course, when they again turn up on your front doorstep, pretending to care about whatever it is that concerns you.

There was a brief time when I wondered if I should also learn to mouth platitudes and lie until I'm blue in the face when I left school – in other words, become a politician. Was that the only way I could do something about climate change?

I knew what such a move would entail. It would mean spending years listening to mums complain about our streets being unsafe for children, dads complain about the irregularity of garbage collections or the necessity for a new bypass, families complain about the lack of council services considering the high rates they had to pay, and old dears like gran complain about the lack of amenities for senior citizens. My constituents wouldn't be in the slightest bit interested to know how I felt about global warming. Nor, for that matter, about the Israel-Palestinian conflict, Syria, Yemen, Iran, Afghanistan or North Korea.

My chances of becoming a politician who was able to do something about the really important stuff was zero. Or less. Anyway, by the time I reached the exalted heights of Prime Minister of my country, like our current Prime Moron, it's likely the world will have ended. The matter's far too urgent for me to harbour political ambitions. Also, there's the slight problem that I'm not even eligible to vote yet.

Once, I considered writing a book about climate change. Do a Rachel Carson, so to speak. But compared to back then, we're now drowning in books. Experts churn out books and articles on global warming faster than people can read them. Millions of acres of forest are doubtless pulped in order to publish them all – nature destroyed in order to defend nature. Sure, some of the books briefly cause a stir before sinking quietly into oblivion, but they're the exception. Most just disappear, unread.

Writing a book won't get me anywhere, so I'll have to make do with getting my thoughts down on paper for you. Maybe there's some kind of satisfaction to be had from convincing one person – like you, Dr. C., should you ever read this – that caring about the environment doesn't mean a person's insane.

Of course, the real reason you think I'm crazy – if you do – is because I did take action against climate change. And look where it got me. Apart from being locked up in this madhouse – which should rightfully be the home of all our politicians – I'm not sure I've achieved any-thing by doing something. I see now that what I did was a complete waste of time, too insignificant to count. Yet it would still have been insane to do nothing.

Every now and then, during those three hours of waiting, one of the lifts would descend to the car park and someone would step out and head for their car. We collectively held our breath as each person appeared, but as they headed off to some distant part of the under-ground car park, we would all sigh audibly in unison. The majority of the staff with cars came within the first hour.

After about 7pm, fewer people appeared. We were worried by a car that was parked three or four spaces from the van – a sleek Jag. We guessed it belonged to a director who was probably still at his desk. We realised that if anyone was to take a look inside our van, it would most likely be him. We alternately prayed that he'd go home soon (then we'd be rid of him), and prayed that he wouldn't leave (in case he discovered us in the van).

The lift doors in the basement car park eventually opened, and a woman came out. She was wearing a suit and was carrying a slim briefcase. She walked straight towards us. 'Oh shit, it's the Jaguar owner, if I'm not mistaken,' whispered Dougal.

I lay down on the front seat (how was I going to explain if the woman knocked on the window?! 'Oh, I'm just having a kip before I go up and see my dad.') We lay in shadow, and held our collective breath. We listened to her approach, her heels loud on the bare concrete. Then we heard the beep as she unlocked her car, the door open, then close. A minute later, she drove off.

I THINK IT WAS THE NEXT TIME I SAW YOU THAT YOU ASKED me about my mum. Fair enough, I suppose, seeing that we'd already discussed dad.

I find the start of these sessions a bit awkward, TBH. I need time to warm up. I remember taking a quick look round the room, which was no help at all. I know it too well, and it's boring. Not even a window to look out of. Just you sitting on your leather and chrome rocking chair, me on the sofa. A desk somewhere beneath stacks of files, a half-buried computer, a phone (that never seems to ring) and lots of other stuff. Innocuous paintings on the wall, forgettable curtains, nothing to distract anyone, not even the desperately bored.

'She's unreal,' I said.

You said nothing. I felt compelled to try and fill the silence. 'She's like someone you might read about in the pages of a novel. She has a kind of fictional reality, if that makes sense to you.' I'm not sure that it did to me.

'Is she glamorous, is that what you mean?'

'Definitely. Yes. She was born with a silver spoon in her mouth. Good family and all that – far better than dad's...' I was waffling.

You have this effect on me: I want to appear more interesting than I am, like I don't want to risk boring you. I'm aware of this, even though I don't know why I should react in such a way. But I can't discuss that with you, obviously.

You were frowning at me – about the most expressive you ever allow yourself to be – like you wanted me to explain. 'I'm not sure what I meant by that. Sorry...'

'There's no need to feel sorry.'

I shrugged.

'I think she's more interested in herself than anyone else, if that makes sense.'

Another painful pause. 'She's always going on about these being the best years of my life, and looking all wistful and nostalgic when she says it, like she'd step into my shoes immediately given half a chance. She certainly has no idea about the pressure I'm under from dad right now to get into uni. I spend my life studying – except when I'm wasting my time in here.'

(I couldn't resist that, but you ignored the comment anyway.)

'It's like she doesn't think exams are important in the grand scheme of things. Try telling that to my dad, or to Mr. Marshall!'

'Mr. Marshall?'

'Our head.'

You nodded vaguely. 'Are you sure that's how she feels?'

'I'm sure. Take global warming. Same thing. She has no idea how worried I am about that – totally oblivious. She said to me recently: "Oh, let's not talk about that, darling."'

'Global warming?'

I nodded. '"It's too unpleasant," she said. "At least we're not all dead yet." At which point she probably poured herself another sherry.'

'Does your sister feel the same way towards your mother?'

'I guess so. They certainly don't go in for those mother and daughter deep and meaningfuls, which I think they're supposed to. Sam's always telling mum to grow up and take responsibility for her life – to get real is how she puts it. She once told her to embrace feminism. Which was a bit weird considering neither of them is ever likely to head off in that direction.'

'Why is that?'

'Dad would prove to be a considerable hurdle between mum and feminism. I think he'd probably divorce her before allowing her to pass down that path.'

'I see.'

That's your favourite expression: 'I see.' I wonder if you do. Your other favourite is, 'How do you feel about that?' I like you though, despite that. Unlike most grown-ups, you listen to what I say – and yes, I know you're paid to, but still... You're just not very open, you know, not easy to talk to.

You rarely speak, for instance. Just like the Buddha (or that's how I imagine he was, rarely speaking). You remind me of the Buddha, that's why I said that. You're kind of small and round like him, and I never have any idea what you're thinking. If I ask you a question, you throw it straight back at me.

'Why do I hate my father?' I ask.

'Why do you think you hate him, Alan?' is your reply. Helpful, what!

'I don't. Not really.'

In the last session I didn't get around to telling you how my friends always seem to be so full of hope and optimism. Zoe in particular. She kind of goes through life with her arms spread wide, like she's embracing every experience that comes her way, even global warming and end of year exams. I like that about her. I'm envious of that ability. It's an anything-is-possible outlook on life, the-world-is-our-oyster approach to existence.

Her scenario has a Romantic feel to it. It feels like

sylvan meadows, blooming daffodils, birds tweeting (before the word was hijacked by Silicon Valley), couples wandering hand in hand, or studying their tablets and laptops in the dappled shade of spreading oak trees. That's how her attitude to life sounds to me.

And what's wrong with that? It's an idyll (as well as an ideal), but it's unrealistic. It might be like life at Oxford, Cambridge, Yale or Harvard – and, sure, I'd love to attend any of those universities – but it's a representation of how life *should* be; a time given over to finer things, like love, nature and books. It's not how life *is*. Life is oil spills, coal mine disasters, and nuclear explosions…

Something I did say to you – or at least I think I did (I find it hard recalling what I say in our sessions) – was how I see my reality.

'I'm sixteen,' I said. 'My place in this world is midway between childhood and adulthood. The truth is, I missed out on childhood, and adulthood looks increasingly as if it's going to be either cut short or terribly compromised.'

You probably had a questioning look on your face, like you wanted me to expand on what I'd said, but don't want to ask me to, for some reason known only to yourself. 'It's what's been handed down to me by my dad's generation, by the dreaded Baby Boomers.

'The world I've been born into is dying.' I hoped I wasn't sounding too melodramatic. 'I'm not talking about my privileged existence. I'd be more than happy if that went the way of the dinosaur. I'm talking about our planet. It's being killed by my parents, by their friends and colleagues, by politicians and bureaucrats, by... by... by adults. That's my inheritance – a dying world.

'These people, these adults, and they include my own family, have *stolen my childhood*. Mr. Gibson, my English teacher, would say that was a cliché and put a big red cross against it, but I don't know how else to express it.

'It's as if all of the adults in the world are so relaxed about stuffing up the planet, they have no intention of doing anything to protect us. They simply can't be bothered to try and put it right again. Either they won't, or they can't. I'm not sure which it is, to be honest.'

'Are you sure it's as bad as you say?'

'I am, yes. Despite warnings from every scientific and environmental expert in the world, nothing is done. It's like the whole world is deaf and blind, and everyone is hoping the disaster won't happen after all, or they'll be dead before it does, or maybe the experts have got the figures wrong. How else can you explain this mind-boggling lack of action?'

And after offloading myself of all of this – which is really important to me, you know, meaningful – I looked at you, Dr. C, and you were just nodding. Looking thoughtful while you nodded, but basically just waiting for me to spill some more. No comment in other words. Not an iota of sympathy or understanding – although I can't believe that's true.

It must be that they won't put it right, that's what I think. I'm stunned by the indifference of those in public life when it comes to global warming. They don't seem to care one way or the other about the fate of our planet, and I find it hard to know what to do in the face of such apathy and indifference.

The world – *my* world – is scorched by drought and fires, flooded by hurricanes, typhoons and melting ice caps, and made almost uninhabitable by the burning of fossil fuels and the raping of the land by gigantic agricultural concerns. That's my inheritance.

I'm living what mum insists on calling the best years of my life in an environmental firestorm. It's like having a birthday party on the crazily sloping decks of the *Titanic*.

And mum and dad, like everyone else, are sitting in their armchairs reading, or watching TV, or tracking their share portfolios. They're absolutely indifferent to the fate that's about to befall their children. Maybe they know they won't be around long enough to witness the final act, so they've left the theatre early, maybe during the interval. The second half isn't worth seeing is how they excuse their behaviour to Sam and me. Even though we're screaming in terror, they do not seem to notice. And if they do, they are obviously not fazed.

The only answer that springs to my mind is to escape into space, to another planet, to a planet not yet fucked up by us – by Homo hahaha Sapiens. To do an Elon Musk or Richard Branson. Unfortunately, unlike them, we don't have deep enough pockets to entertain such a possibility. Anyway, if those two gentlemen ever manage to reach some pristine planet or other, they will immediately fuck that up as well. That's what they do for a living, that's what the whole world does for a living: fuck things up.

What do you suggest, Dr. Craig? Is it possible to escape my doomed inheritance? It doesn't seem possible to me. We can't flee because there's nowhere to flee to. There's nowhere we'll be safe. We're not even safe in our own home.

I read somewhere that in the not-too-distant future the world will be split into two camps: the rich and the poor (mum and dad will be in the former, no doubt about that). There'll be more poor people than rich people, obviously. I won't repeat all those statistics about a miniscule percentage of the world's population owning an obscenely disproportionate percentage of the world's wealth, or possessing the equivalent of the combined GDPs of hundreds of countries. I'm sure you've heard them all before. But I can't resist giving you one stat:

The *eight* richest men in the world have the same wealth as the poorest *four billion* (well, 3.7 if you want to be exact). That's pretty staggering, don't you think? An individual being richer than a whole country is just mind-boggling when you really think about it.

In the future, poor people will be forced to live in the areas most affected by climate change – in the swamps, marshes and flood-prone areas. They won't be able to afford to live anywhere else. Almost all of these areas will be in the southern hemisphere, which has done little to cause global warming, but will suffer most severely from it.

The northern hemisphere, which caused the majority of the atmospheric damage in the first place, won't be affected anywhere near as bad. How unfair is that!

Many of the poor will have to move away from their homes, from the places where they were born – like the Pacific Islands and the Amazon. They'll have a hard time finding work. Any work they do find will be menial, and involve working either directly or indirectly for the rich.

It will be a bit like the way Palestinians now pour into Israel every day to do the cleaning, washing, labouring and repair jobs, anything menial that the Israelis feel is beneath them.

The poor will be paid very little, a barely liveable wage with which they will have to support their families. They'll always be hungry, thirsty (fresh water will be at a premium), too hot or too cold, and will only ever have a shack to shelter in – if they're lucky. It will be a minimal existence, scraping together the bare essentials to stay alive, and being told how grateful they should be for the little they receive.

Meanwhile, the rich (according to this article) will live a reasonable life in this crippled world they themselves created. They'll have enough money to build their homes on higher ground, beyond the rising sea levels, and will get first pick of the crops that are harvested on the limited ground that's still productive. They'll be the only ones who can afford such luxuries. They'll also have enough money to access the little water that's still drinkable – at the expense of everyone else, of course. The rich will have work, and will earn enough money to afford to eat and drink – even if extremely modestly. And they'll be able to live and sleep in relatively comfortable houses.

The rich obviously have more to lose, but only because they had more to begin with. Which explains why they don't want to do anything now: they want to hang on to what they have for as long as possible. The poor have little to lose when the effects of global warming become truly unbearable, because they have so little now.

But when the planet eventually goes to shit, it strikes me that everyone, rich and poor, will end up equal. Together at the bottom of the pile, without anyone at all at the top. Jeff Bezos will live next door to the person who collects his garbage. Climate change will be the great leveler.

How will my parents cope in this future? They probably won't have to. They probably won't be around then. More to the point, how will I cope?

I don't think I'll have what it takes. I'm not sure I could fend off thirst-crazed crowds from my water supply (if I have one) with a rifle. Or slash at people with a machete when they try to steal my vegetables (if I have some). Or stab anyone who seeks shelter in my hut (if

I have one). I'm not convinced I could do any of that, even if it meant my own survival.

I find it hard to understand why we're heading for such a world. We set out on this journey many decades ago, and are now nearing our destination. But there have been plenty of warnings along the way, so why are we continuing to go down this particular path?

Perhaps you can answer that question for me, Dr. Craig.

I'M INCREASINGLY CONVINCED THAT YOU'RE NEVER GOING to read this. I think that's good. If I'm just writing for myself, it's much easier to put down on paper what's going through my mind. If I'm worrying about what the person leaning over my shoulder is thinking, it's harder to tell the truth.

I wonder how long you intend to keep me in here. Or is it more a question of how long is my father going to keep me in here?

See, I'm not even sure who my warders are.

FOR ME, THE FINAL STRAW WAS THE COALMINE — ALTHOUGH in the end it proved not to be the *final* final straw. Politicians gave the go-ahead to what was to be the biggest coalmine in the southern hemisphere, like that was something to be proud of. It was bitter news, and left me (and thousands, if not millions, of others) without hope.

It was like those in charge were saying, not only do we have the most destructive bomb in the world, but we're going to drop it right on top of our own country, on the heads of our own citizens.

How good is that, Mr. Prime Moron, how good is that! (That's the idiotic expression our head of government uses when he's announcing something that sane people think is really bad news.)

The years of environmental protests and arguments against the coalmine were simply brushed aside. I'm pleased it wasn't a new oil well, of course. That would have been too close to home. I wouldn't have wanted to come up so directly against dad, even though I suspect he thinks I crossed the line a long time ago.

According to the Government, this proposed coalmine promises lots of good things for our country: more coal for export to other countries (so we can pollute them as well), more jobs for our country, and, of course, more votes for their own Party. Personally, I doubt the extra votes they hope to buy by approving this mine will ever materialise because, by the time the next election rolls around, most of the electorate will probably have died from inhaling coal dust. But that's just my prediction.

What they don't mention is how most of the profits will head overseas, and that the increase in the number of jobs will be both minimal and temporary. I also cannot find any information from the government about the increase in pollution, the raising of CO2 emissions, the additional health problems for the locals, and the huge environmental damage – to the water table, the local fauna, and the Reef.

Of course, they attempted to downplay the environmental damage by publishing *expert* scientific studies written by *world-renowned* specialists. Yes, right! These malleable, consciousness-less (is there such a word?) and biased scientists doubtless received substantial monetary rewards for their trouble.

Although Zoe was happy to sign the petition against the coalmine *for my sake*, she insisted that she wasn't going to become involved with the controversy. Like most people, I suppose. 'You know, Al,' she whispered sweetly (I think she may even have been nibbling my ear as she said this), 'it may be a good thing for a lot of people, for jobs, and the economy, and for the…' She seemed to run out of inspiration at that stage.

When I asked her about the damage to the water table and the coastal reefs, she looked blank. After a rather long silence, she assured me, with a carefree shake of her flaming hair, 'Well, perhaps you're right. What do I know?' She giggled. 'But I'm sure it won't be that bad. They wouldn't go ahead with it if it was. They're not stupid, you know.' (Wow! It was such a naïve comment, I couldn't bring myself to say anything that might disillusion her.)

I loved her though, despite her being into Justin Bieber, and despite us not always agreeing on everything. The problem is, she always wanted to agree with me, as if that would please me (which it didn't), and it was like she made this incredible effort to go along with whatever I said, no matter how dumb it might have been. She thought I was clever, so maybe that's all it was – like she didn't feel she could argue with me because I knew better. I wasn't happy about that. It wasn't like I wanted to argue with her, not at all, I just think it's healthy to have different opinions on things now and again. It doesn't mean you don't love each other.

Perhaps you're right after all, Dr. C. Perhaps I am mad. I was certainly mad about Zoe.

I've never felt this way about anyone else, that's for sure, and I had such dreams for us. She was so natural, so open, so generous, and she let me go further than any other girl I've been out with. It was like she wanted to give me a present of herself, like it would make me happy (which it certainly would have done), so why did I continue to say no?

I was always telling her that we had to be sure before we went all the way, we both had to be fully committed, and she looked at me like she didn't understand what I was talking about. She was happy to go all the way right away, that's what she told me, and she also told me she wasn't a virgin, so why did I hesitate, why did I refuse her? Especially when I loved her. I wonder if it was because I suspected she would be happy to make a present of herself to other boys too, and for the same reason – to make them happy. So her feelings for me might not be any stronger than her feelings for other blokes.

I shouldn't say things like that. I know it's not true.

It does my head in, it really does. Maybe I should talk to you about this, find out what you think. You must be talking about peoples' relationships all the time.

We went to a party a few months ago, before I came in here. It was at the home of some boy she goes to school with. We were both a bit out of it to tell the truth, so it probably wasn't the best time to tell her I was in love with her. Anyway, I did, and she grinned at me, her freckled nose wrinkling up like it does when she's amused by something.

'Why are you laughing?' I was a little hurt, because I was for real.

'Because you're stating the obvious, Al,' she said. 'Of course you love me, of course I love you.' She was so earnest when she said that. 'Why else are we going out together? I'm not going out with anyone else, you know? I wouldn't go out with you if I didn't love you.'

And she kissed me, like to prove the truth of what she was saying, and – excuse me telling you this – but I got the biggest hard-on I've ever had. Not because of the kiss, but because of what she'd said, the words. And I was suddenly so crazily in love with her, I was really tempted to take her upstairs and find a bedroom, and go all the way, right there and then.

But I didn't. And yes, I know, I'm an idiot. Especially when it all went haywire just a few weeks later.

I KNOW YOU'RE GIVING ME MEDICATION, OF COURSE I DO.

But it's medication to stop me being insane, whereas I think you should be giving me medication to stop me being angry. I'm not completely sure about that to tell the truth, about wanting to lose my anger. I think the cause deserves nothing less. I must maintain the rage if I'm to achieve anything, if I'm to destroy the destroyers of our world. It worries me that you're also giving me something to calm me down. Although I want to calm down a little, I don't want it to be at the expense of my anger. I don't want to be *that* calm.

We've discussed this before – many times – and you always smile at me benignly, as if I don't know what I'm talking about. And yes, I understand your problem: everyone in this facility (I can't bring myself to call it a home) must claim to be sane (although surely not Alastair, the crazy masturbator), so why should you believe my claims to sanity over those of others?

Mum came to see her environ-*mental* son this afternoon. Ha ha ha, that's funny. Dad hasn't yet visited me – which is a bit of a relief, to be honest. What would we talk about? He would probably spend the visit lecturing me on how I had to work harder at school, and not waste time on 'idiot projects' like climate change. But I'd still like to see him though – which probably surprises you.

'He's very busy, darling. He's leaving for the Middle East tomorrow. You know your father.'

She was wrong. I don't think I do.

Does mum think I'm mad? I'm not sure, but I suspect she avoids answering that question by never asking it. I'm convinced she sees me more as a social embarrassment. (I wonder how she explains my absence to her friends. *He's visiting friends overseas*, or some such ridiculous lie.)

She was quite tearful at times during the visit, but I felt this was put on for my benefit, like she thought I expected it of her. I didn't. I have absolutely no recollection of mum ever crying (except when she's drunk too much), so I have to admit I was a little taken aback when I caught a glimpse of what may have been a tear in the corner of one eye. She dabbed at it quickly with a handkerchief.

I felt this wasn't because she wished to hide the tear from me, but because she was afraid I'd be disappointed by the lack of volume, by her failure to produce more. That probably sounds cynical to you, but I don't mean it to. It's simply how I felt, that my mother's tear, or tears (could there have been two?) lacked sincerity.

At one stage she said, 'I'm sure your father knows best, darling.' She meant that my being in this clinic, surrounded by eye-rolling, muttering, masturbating and twitching companions, was appropriate, even suitable. 'Your father knows best' was her answer to most of the difficult questions in her life, so I wasn't in the least surprised by her statement. It certainly wasn't worth arguing about.

Both of my parents are seriously conservative. They're scared of what will happen if they step outside the status quo. They cling to the way of life they know, even though I think it makes them really unhappy, and because they're worried about what they might lose.

The other thing mum said was, 'His grandfather had mental health issues, you know...' Although her comment lacked detail, I made no effort to dig deeper. I knew she was simply trying to inform me that my supposed 'problems' were hereditary, and not from her side of the family. By my mother's habitual sit-on-the-fence standards it was an impressive betrayal.

She was looking askance at my fellow patients throughout her visit, her alarm meant to convey that such behaviour was absolutely foreign to her. She didn't hug me when she left, although she did manage to give my hand an affectionate squeeze.

Preciate.

I PULLED UP MY FACE MASK AS I APPROACHED THE LIFT, BUT kept my head down. It was about 9pm when I pressed the button for the Ground Floor. If I ran into anyone, I had no stronger alibi than to say I was dropping a document off for my father (having already, hopefully, whipped off my mask). It sounded unbelievable, unlikely and completely naïve, and I felt sick at the prospect of having to use it.

I pressed up against the side of the lift as the door opened, and peered cautiously out. The reception area was about the size of a soccer pitch. It was dimly lit and had a scattering of leather armchairs. Behind the desk there was subdued lighting. There was no one in sight, and no sign of any cleaners. I stayed in the lift and went back down to the Basement.

'It looks clear, but there must be cleaners up there on one of the floors. One of the lifts is stuck on the ninth floor, so they're probably up there. It's hard to tell.'

Dougal and Matt put on their masks and climbed out of the back of the van. They were wearing white lab coats – although none of us believed they'd carry much weight with Security late in the evening in a closed office. They struggled to lift the barrel of oil out of the van and onto the trolley we'd brought with us. Keeping close to the wall, Dougal pushed it towards the lift, closely followed by Matt and myself. We'd already decided that all three of us should go up. We hoped to be in and out within a few minutes.

When the doors opened, Dougal and Matt stepped out into Reception, while I kept my finger on the button to prevent the doors closing. With impressive speed, the two men pushed the barrel onto the carpet, unscrewed the cap on top, tipped it over, and rolled it rapidly across the room.

Almost panic-stricken, I stared at the huge plate glass window fronting onto the street, but was unable to see if there were any passers-by, or know if they'd be able to see what was happening on our side of the glass.

The black viscous liquid was spurting out of the mouth of the barrel, pulsing out in thick globules as it rolled. At the far end of the room, the two men quickly spun it around and rolled it back over the untouched parts of the carpet. Then suddenly, quite unexpectedly, they hefted it up onto the mahogany reception desk and splashed the remainder of the contents across the length of it. They hadn't told me they were going to do that, and for some reason, it freaked me out completely. It struck me as too extreme.

Carefully avoiding stepping in the slowly spreading trail of oil, they stood the empty barrel upright, and Dougal took a sheet of paper from inside his white coat and placed it on top of the barrel. I already knew what it said: 'FUCK YOUR ENVIRONMENT TOO.'

Then, as if they'd decided on this particular course of action earlier between themselves, they undid their overalls and pissed on the parts of the carpet that weren't already covered in oil. The way they turned left and right, spraying near and far – remember, we'd been in the van for almost four hours – horrified me. I'm not sure why, perhaps because it was like adding insult to injury. But I said nothing when they got back in the lift. They were laughing their heads off, so what was the point? As we descended to the car park, Dougal whispered, 'Well done, lads.' And it was like he'd taken over, like he was now the boss.

'Let's not congratulate each other until we've left the building,' I said.

I was worried – and maybe the other two also – about whether or not the parking pass would open the gate –

would it work as it had on the way in? There wasn't any reason why it shouldn't, but… I had nightmares about being locked in the building.

It worked.

The next day it was all over the internet, as well as the TV and newspapers. There were also grainy shots of the masked and hooded Dougal and Matt in the reception area, and of our van in the car park. We'd agreed not to be in touch with each other for at least a week, so I had no idea how concerned they were by these shots.

Their arrest was reported in the media the following day. I expected the police to knock on my door within hours. I waited and waited… Sam continually asking me why I was so twitchy – 'Is it that time of the month?' She could be so annoying.

I knew my arrest was inevitable. We obviously weren't very successful environmental activists.

'IF WE KEEP YOU HERE FOR A WHILE, ALAN' (DURATION STILL unspecified, I noted), 'I think we should be able to stop you obsessing about climate change.'

You were staring at me meaningfully, as if you were secretly telling me where I could find the key to the front door. 'You must learn to relax and stop fretting.'

I like you, Dr. Craig, although I have to admit I don't have much faith in this therapy thing. For instance, I seem to be growing more fearful with every day that passes. Every day I question why nothing is being done about climate change. It's driving me nuts. (*Sane boy goes insane in mental home.*)

I read recently about how all the talk in the media about global warming is making a lot of people depressed, even suicidal. I totally get that. I feel the same.

It's been building steadily since Hugh asked me that question about how I felt about dad's work. And I can't even get that post-election rally out of my head. I see the scene so clearly, and it plays over and over and over in my mind like some sick nightmare.

I'm repeatedly forced to view the cheering, banner and flag waving supporters. The newly elected leader is up on stage with his family and Party bigwigs. There's a lot of back-slapping, and self-congratulatory hugging. They're all so pleased with themselves, so complacent, it makes me want to puke. They've just been voted in for a second term, to carry on as before – to basically do nothing about 'the greatest moral challenge of our time'. I guess that's why dad keeps on toasting them with gin and tonics from the depths of the sofa.

Leading up to the election, they told voters that jobs and economic growth were more important than dealing with climate change (which, as far as I can make out, doesn't exist according to them, so I suppose that makes it easier for them to do nothing).

'They repeat the same mantra endlessly,' Hugh said when we were watching the News at his place one evening before the election. 'We must go for growth,' he mimicked, 'because growth means money… and more money means more jobs… and more jobs mean we enjoy a better lifestyle, and…'

'They're like a stuck record,' I said.

But the voters seemingly agreed with the Prime Moron and his party, the election result showing that the majority of the country were more interested in their hip pocket than in the future of the human race. So much for democracy! It means we can look forward to three or four more years (however long it is between elections) of the same tosspots continuing to bury their heads in the sand, and deny global warming.

The party leader has his wife and kids up on stage with him (even though it must be long past their bedtime). His nearest and dearest obviously haven't been told about the recent catastrophic rise in CO2 emissions because they're all grinning ear-to-ear like they've just managed to jump onto the most humungous gravy train ever.

Perhaps the head of the family hasn't yet told them that he isn't going to do anything about the CO2 emissions in our country, just as he's probably forgotten to spill the beans about the world coming to an end. It must have slipped his mind.

He may be under the misapprehension that his kids will survive somehow, and that his grandkids, should they eventually arrive, will also get by. They'll find food and water in the parched landscape, find shelter from the burning sun – beneath a cheap umbrella maybe –

and be provided with a small boat when the sea floods the land.

Those are the kind of nonsensical – as in insane – benefits of being the country's leader.

I wonder if the Prime Moron and his Party are selfish, or if they're simply stupid – or stupidly simple. I can't stop myself thinking about that. It has to be one or the other, surely? I'm not even certain which is preferable.

If they're stupid, it's because they don't understand the mechanics of global warming. I admit it's pretty complicated. Sometimes I feel I don't have a really good grasp of the subject myself. But if you're the government, it's surely easy enough to round up a few scientific eggheads and have them brief you in words of one or two syllables, Janet- and John-type language – perhaps with a PowerPoint presentation using a few easy-to-follow pictures.

The problem is, the fossil fuel lobbyists are doubtless desperate to keep scientists well away from the Prime Moron and his ministers, just in case they grab the opportunity to explain how mankind is fucking up the planet, and why time has almost run out to do anything about it.

However, if the PM and his ministers are selfish rather than stupid – and I'm leaning more in that direction – it's definitely a bigger worry. It means they won't do anything about the climate catastrophe because it benefits them in some way to do nothing. Doing nothing won't benefit the country, but maybe it somehow benefits them and their cronies. Power, influence, their hip pockets, who knows… Trouble is, one will probably never know what motivates them, if indeed they have any motivation at all. I guess that's a third possibility…

The way the Prime Moron is forever whipping out lumps of coal in Parliament and shouting 'won't hurt you, won't hurt you,' could mean he carries loads of the stuff around on his person: in his pockets or briefcase. Oil as well, perhaps – in the boot of his car, his garden shed or his bathtub. He could be stashing away fossil fuels as some kind of future nest egg for himself and his family.

Both scenarios – stupidity and selfishness – are doubtless possible. I'm unable to think of any other explanation for these idiots to sit around on their hands all day, doing nothing. But wait a minute! Our head of government's a Christian of some kind or other, so maybe he's keen to bring about the end of the world. Perhaps he can't wait to shake off this mortal coil (or whatever Bill Shakespeare said) and go and join the Good Lord in Paradise.

A bit off the wall maybe, but I think that might explain everything. He could be carrying out the Lord's work, hallelujah! Praying that coal and oil will bring about the Second Coming, hallelujah! When the world is finally destroyed, the true believers will rise up and be saved. Praise the Lord and pass the fossil fuels!

(It's *alarming* the way so many right-wing climate

deniers, like our blokey, hail-fellow-well-met suburban Prime Moron, are getting the top jobs in so many countries around the world. It really makes me wonder how such movements come about. I must ask Mr. Webb, our history teacher about it. That is, if you ever release me from this place, and if I ever get to see Mr. Webb again.)

The future looks so bleak, I'm sometimes unable to see myself ever getting out of here. I'm falling behind with school work. I try to study a bit, but it's not nearly enough. I seem incapable of setting my mind to anything right now. Hardly anyone comes to visit me anymore. Mainly just mum, Sam and Hugh. It's beginning to get me down. I sometimes wish it would end.

I'm not going to mention this to you, Dr. Craig. First, because I probably won't do anything about it. And second because you'd probably put me in a padded cell, and take away my shoelaces, belt and tie.

I'm more than willing to die for the cause, to lay down my life in the battle against climate change. It would be so much better than living here, in this prison. I feel incapable of achieving anything worthwhile in the battle to save the planet, so completely out of my depth that I feel compelled to make some kind of statement – a worthwhile statement. Such a statement might be considered an achievement.

I feel I've had enough. I could leave a message for my parents, even though they'll probably be too busy to read it. Or I could leave a message for the government. I don't mean I'd take an overdose and leave a message for the Prime Moron by my bedside. It would never get to him, and if it did, as likely as not he'd take a leaf out of my parents' book and not bother to read it. Or I could write directly to the Media. That might work. *16-year old's suicide note to a dying world* has a certain appeal.

If I commit suicide, it should be spectacular. You have to be spectacular or outrageous to get hits on the Internet nowadays, otherwise no one pays any attention to them. I should carry it out in the capital, the seat of Government. It's a dead place (all concrete, pillars and steps), full of dead people (politicians of all persuasions), so it seems kind of apt.

An act of terrorism is my first thought. Like a car bomb. I've come to understand why people commit acts of terror, why they become suicide bombers. It's about the only way to make people sit up and listen to what you have to say. But I'm not that keen on killing innocent people, unlike our climate-denying politicians (who are, let's face it, basically mass-murderers). I wouldn't object to killing a minister or two, but think it might be too hard to bring about with all those security thugs surrounding them twenty-four seven.

But if I was to carry out my own murder correctly, it might make people sit up and pay attention. There would be lots of Media coverage (if only because I'm my father's son), and they'd likely publish any message I left behind about global warming.

I should hire a car and drive as close as I can to the Parliament. There are guards everywhere, so I'll have to choose my spot carefully. Douse myself in petrol inside the vehicle, walk quickly to some central spot, hopefully as far as possible from any cops or fire extinguishers. How long will I have? How long will it take for me to die? I know I have to die (that's what makes the event spectacular), but I'm a coward and I don't want to suffer. I certainly don't want someone to extinguish the flames while I'm still alive. I don't want to survive with fourth-degree burns. That would be grotesque.

Maybe I should carry a can of petrol with me, and open it just before I set myself alight. It would explode then, and that would feed the fire as well as kill me. I have to make sure that the flames are visually impressive, and hope that someone photographs me – a tourist, I guess. That's the only way I'd get in the papers or on Instagram: death by fossil fuels. Death by my father's livelihood. Death of the oil man's son.

Perhaps I should discuss this with you after all. But I'd worry that you'd immediately think I should stay in here even longer. Of course, if you ever get around to reading this, and I don't expect you will, then you can make the decision for me – whether or not I should end it all.

The other option is to fill Sam's car with cans of petrol (without asking her, of course), and drive it smack into a public building. Cause a huge explosion.

My only worry is that I'll come across as some kind of lunatic, like one of those freaks who shoot up high schools in America. After the slaughter, the TV stations invariably film the cops in a suburban street, usually in front of the killer's weeping, mystified parents, and the head cop is always saying something about the perpetrator of the mass shooting being a hater of some group or other (Jews, Muslims, Christians, Blacks, Whites, Queers), and how he was a member of the Extreme Right, Extreme Left or Extreme Centre who thinks his country is fucked, that he was convinced he alone had the solution to its problems, and that it was his God-given right to bear arms and shoot as many people as he wanted before he himself was martyred by law enforcement officers.

Then they interview a few of the neighbours, all of whom always say exactly the same thing: 'Such a quiet boy… Ever so polite… Always smiled and said good morning if you passed him in the street… Many times I saw him help old folks across the road…' Blah, blah, blah!

I must check with Hugh again that he and I aren't lunatics (coming out when the moon waxes and wanes)! It increasingly worries me. I don't think we are, but then I don't suppose the men who slaughter innocent schoolkids think they're lunatics either. They just think they're right – like me. That's the problem. I think I'm right, and it's the clowns in government who are wrong.

Although this is obvious to me, I have to ask if *you* think I'm not right in the head – a real nutter. I have to ask because I'm pretty sure every mental patient last thing at night must tell himself the same thing: *I'm not mad.*

I'M NOT SURE — IT'S ALL A LITTLE VAGUE NOW — BUT SAM may have used the word 'sorry' when she apologised for betraying me. If she did, that would have been quite something.

I've noticed how those in authority are always being asked to say 'Sorry' nowadays, yet hardly ever do so. If the original settlers of a country are upset by the way history has treated them, or men or women decide they were abused by their church when they were kids, or governments of an earlier century didn't do the right thing by the people they were governing, then today's leaders — when trying to right the wrongs of long ago — are expected to eat humble pie. To abase themselves.

They can't get away with, 'We regret what happened a hundred years ago,' or 'We humbly apologise for any hurt this organisation may have caused in the past.'

Nothing like that. No, no, no! They must use that magic word, *sorry*: 'I'm sorry we did whatever you're accusing us of having done all those decades ago.' I can never work out why that word is so significant, why it carries so much more weight than all of those other words of contrition, but it does.

What I'm getting at is, I think I'm due a 'Sorry' (and I'm not asking for one from Sam and Zoe, even though they could learn a lesson from this). I'm due a 'Sorry' along with everyone else on the planet. Yes, my generation and all future generations are absolutely due a big, loud 'Sorry!'

It's time for the heads of every government to stand before its citizens – no, maybe spread-eagle themselves in the dirt like monks applying for holy orders (I seem to remember that's what they do) – and say that one word.

Sorry we fucked up your country, your world, and your future.

Sorry you and your children won't actually have a future because we did nothing to solve the problems of climate change.

Sorry my government turned you all into dead men walking.

That would be a real feel-good moment, even though a fat lot of good it would do any of us.

No one has ever apologised to me, or regretted what happened in the past, let alone said sorry. So why don't I take them to court? That's what a lot of people do now: take the State, or the Church, or a business, or whoever to court. Sue them for millions.

'You've screwed up my life, now pay me compensation. And maybe you should also pay for my funeral.'

But it doesn't seem like it would achieve very much, like it would be worth doing.

My father called the day after Dougal and Matt were arrested, from Houston. I saw 'Dad' come up on my phone. I closed my eyes. I hesitated. I had no idea what I should do. He rang off. What a relief! A second later, he rang back. I was tempted not to answer, but knew I'd have to speak to him eventually. I also knew that he'd already spoken to mum. (I'd heard her say, 'Oh my God!' and nothing else, several times down the phone. I also heard her go to the drinks' cabinet. She sounded traumatised, and that told me everything I needed to know. They now knew.)

'Hi dad!' It wasn't easy to sound cheerful in the circumstances.

'What on earth were you thinking, Alan?'

Those were his first words. There wasn't much point trying to delay matters by asking him what he meant by them, although I had no idea what I could say in reply.

'Your co-conspirators dobbed you in,' he said, obviously intent on demoralising me straight off. I knew it must have been hard to get through the long police interviews without cracking, so although I wasn't happy about it, I wasn't exactly surprised that I'd been included in their confession.

I still said nothing. So he filled the gap in the conversation by telling me that he'd managed (through his lawyers and various high-powered friends) to convince the police to quietly drop any action against me. It seems there was no CTV footage of me in the Reception area, and so the police were persuaded to build their case against Dougal and Matt alone.

'It wasn't easy to persuade the Company's Board to

press charges against only two of the perpetrators. They are justifiably furious at your criminal and irresponsible behaviour.'

I muttered 'Sorry, dad', or something along those lines, every now and again. And he did make me feel sorry. He was my dad after all, and I'd done completely the wrong thing by him.

He sighed like it was all too much. He can't cope with emotional stuff at the best of times. He's uncomfortable with feelings, that's my opinion.

'The only way I could get the Board to back down was to promise them that I would seek suitable treatment for you.' There was a loaded pause. Where was this going? I had no idea, but was filled with foreboding.

'"My son isn't right in the head," I told them. "It's very sad." And I'm afraid that's how I do feel, Alan – that you're not right in the head.'

I confess I wanted to cry at that point. I closed my eyes tight. I suspected mum was lurking on the other side of my bedroom door, trying to hear as much as she could of our conversation, but I couldn't be bothered to look. I wanted to be left alone, to be allowed to curl up and die.

'I'm sorry, dad.'

'So am I, Alan. So am I.'

It was a bit like that Pinter play we put on at school last term – *The Birthday Party*. All pauses... and silences...

'Staff from a rehabilitation centre – 'the best in the

country,' he added, as if that might make it easier for me – will pick you up tomorrow morning, at nine.'

Over the phone, he came across as genuinely concerned. Upset as well, sure, but I was more surprised by how worried he sounded. 'I want to help you,' he said. 'I want to understand your concerns about the environment. I want you to talk to me.'

Then, as if he wanted to end on a stronger, more authoritarian note, he added: 'If you want to avoid going to prison and the ruination of your entire life before it's even started, Alan, not to mention the disgrace you could bring down on your own family, I suggest you accompany them.'

His final words, before he rang off, were, 'Listen to my advice for once.'

The next morning, I went with the two white-coated people (a man and a woman – they obviously weren't expecting me to put up a fight) without causing any problems. I got the impression that it's quite easy to have someone certified so long as you know the right people who'll sign the various forms.

My mother's headache was too severe to allow her to descend from her bedroom to say goodbye, but Sam stood in the entrance and waved cheerfully as we drove off. She obviously thought that her younger brother being taken away to an insane asylum – to a *funny farm* – was a bit of a joke. Hahahaha.

I bet she put it straight up on Facebook.

I'M MAD.

Not like you and dad think I'm mad. Not mad as in crazy. Not mad as in nuts, or sick in the head.

I'm mad as in angry.

Mad as in furious.

Mad as in beside myself. (Where does that come from, 'beside yourself'?)

When I think of what *they* are doing to us, to the world, to our precious planet, to our only home, it makes me sick. And depressed. Locked away in here, I imagine far off places, and how the time will come when it won't be possible to snorkel on the Great Barrier Reef, or cruise beneath the ice cliffs of Antarctica (which I wouldn't do anyway), or walk amongst the giant redwoods of California, or explore the Amazonian jungle, or... They will all be no more.

I want to talk to Zoe about these fears, but she won't listen when I try to explain why I'm upset. She accuses me of always being aggro, and then tells me how *she* is upset because her boyfriend is locked up in a mental institution.

When we last met on the outside – before the Samantha *incident* – she was different. She actually said to me, 'I like it that you have a cause, Al. Most boys only think about sport, or music, or –' she laughed, 'girls. It shows you're passionate. But I don't like it that you're always angry. What good's it doing you, burning up like this? I want you to have a cause that's more fun.'

It was like being awarded a consolation prize at a country fair.

She doesn't take global warming seriously. I'm not convinced she takes anything seriously, that's my impression. She admits the only reason she and her friends went to the schools' demonstration was so they could miss classes. It was probably the reason most people went. Truth is, I went because Hugh's my best friend rather than because of the cause. I didn't tell her that at the time, but maybe I should have done.

Although she can be flippant about the whole climate change thing, she once said something that really made me think. 'You always blame other people about global warming, like coal and oil companies, but what about the part you play?'

'What part do I play?'

'You turn on the lights when you go into a room, Al. You switch on air conditioners when it's too hot or too cold. Everything you buy is wrapped in plastic. You fly in planes. You told me you're hoping your dad will buy you a car when you turn 17...'

She struggled to name other examples at this point (luckily for me!), but after a short pause gave me a quick kiss on the lips, adding: 'So why not do something about your own contribution to climate change instead of complaining about everyone else's? That would be a positive.'

'You're right.' I knew full well she was right. She was 100 per cent right. My ecological footprint was enormous, a great clumsy climate stomp. I was my father's son. Guilty as charged. How could I have not seen it before?

I wondered, if mum and dad did offer to buy me a car for my birthday, would I, could I, say no?

It was like arriving at the station to find the last train has just departed. You still hope – quite unrealistically of course – that perhaps, just this once, there'll be another train along very shortly. It made me despair, really despair. I felt so lonely and helpless. I wish I hadn't found out, that I could have remained ignorant.

This is what happened, what I mentioned earlier in this exercise book. It's time I put it down on paper

Zoe and me planned to meet at my house after school. That's what we arranged. I had to speak to one of the teachers after class about something or other – I can't remember what, but maybe the end of term exams – and I was running late. When I got home, I ran straight upstairs and threw open my bedroom door. It took a few seconds to understand what I was seeing.

Zoe was leaning back against the chest-of-drawers, and her head was so close to Sam's, it was like they were glued together. Tongues were obviously involved. But what really brought me up short was seeing my sister's hand beneath Zoe's school dress and – it was impossible to miss – buried in her knickers, which were pure – yes, *pure* white with some kind of floral motif. (Yes, I'd seen them before, I'd got that far.)

They stopped kissing when I burst in. And Sam reacted like, *bother, we've been interrupted* rather than displaying any kind of guilt at being caught out. It was as if she was simply inconvenienced by my sudden arrival.

I don't know what Zoe was thinking. Sure, she turned her head towards me, but I'm not sure she even saw me. Her eyes were so far back in the top of her head, and she was gasping so loudly it was like she was too busy trying to get air into her lungs to worry about me.

Sam kind of smiled at me slyly. She was very calculating. She didn't look guilty, not even embarrassed, not at all. She didn't move her hand or anything like that, but sort of stared at me like she hoped I could clearly see everything.

I keep on thinking about how Hugh always described Zoe and me as OTP. (That's One True Pairing to you, Dr. Craig.) That's how he felt about us.

Maybe he's not as perceptive as I thought.

There were times when I wanted to scream. Times when I wanted to be sick. Times when I wanted to cry. Before I was locked up in here, every day saw me grow angrier and more depressed.

The anger was real. Like I've never felt before in my life.

Anger that the world was run by complete and utter

fools who were about as far-sighted as moles. (I remember learning in Biology that those creatures are as good as blind.)

Anger at the members of the public who voted for those charlatans in parliament.

Anger that our leaders lacked the courage to speak the words that no one has ever had to speak before in the history of the world: 'We are facing imminent extinction unless we do something immediately.'

Back then, I watched the News compulsively. (I'm not allowed to watch it in here, probably because they think I haven't yet discovered that there are even crazier people outside.) I soaked up endless stories of disasters, half-fascinated, half-appalled, half-disbelieving. (That's too many halves, I know.) It wasn't sensible of me, I was aware of that. The News freaked me out, it stoked my anger. I should have stuck to the commercial stations, which are all about normality and the mundane. They concentrate on rapes, murders and car crashes – ordinary, everyday events that only affect a handful of people, as opposed to all of mankind.

The important news, which grows less important with every year that passes – because it's becoming so commonplace – was about mudslides, landslides, tornadoes and hurricanes, ferocious storms, bursting dams, bridges washed away by floods, forests engulfed in flames, firemen with hoses pissing in the wind, skeletons of cows and sheep on dried, cracked and barren earth. In almost every scene there were people weeping, looking shocked, having lost everything, absolutely everything, they'd ever had.

Apocalyptic news.

There were bushfires everywhere (and I doubt it's changed since I've been in here). Fires in the Americas, in Europe, and throughout Australia (last year's fires releasing almost as much CO_2 as the country's total annual greenhouse gas emissions – which is kind of ironic). Presidents, prime ministers and other mentally-handicapped freaks were flying into these areas in helicopters and looking mystified, like they were surprised by what they were seeing. *Oh my gosh, I never thought…*

These officials experimented with looking compassionate, but any viewer could see that their insincere emotions were overwhelmed by a complete lack of understanding of what was going on. *Crikey, how can this have happened?* they seemed to be asking themselves. *This is as surprising to us as it is to you.* What they were forced to look at was completely alien to what they believed, to the denials they made every day of their lives.

They walked amongst the remains of burnt-out houses, accompanied by the people who once lived there (a blackened child's swing, tricycle or doll usually placed by the cameraman strategically in the background). You could see them trying to commiserate, to look as if they understood what these people were experiencing, but they failed miserably. (Perhaps they don't have feelings.)

The wife of the head honcho would hug any local

woman who came her way and, if she was really on her game, would try and squeeze out a tear or two. Her husband would stick to wringing his hands and frowning a lot, like men do, while he stared resolutely at the ground, probably worried by the ash accumulating on his polished shoes.

'This is a tragedy,' he'd say somberly. This made the locals sit up and listen. Almost certainly, they wouldn't have noticed it was a tragedy until he pointed it out to them. He would then promise financial help, and to pressure the insurance companies to honour all claims quickly. Then he and his wife would fly off home. There they'd knock back a few stiff drinks, and he'd work on some bill or other to be tabled in the House the following day specifically to approve some new coal-fired power station.

There were also regular news stories about floods, often following straight on from a segment on fires in some other part of the world – like some biblical double-whammy. Villages somewhere in Asia had been swept away, along with trees, boulders and cars. In more affluent countries, people sat on suburban rooftops watching helicopters approach to rescue them. Roads everywhere were shown coming to an abrupt halt at the edge of raging torrents.

Every night it was the same story. And increasingly it was met with indifference, with a consensual yawn. It's so yesterday, so expected, so prosaic, so endemic.

The problem is global.

Look at that guy in Brazil. What's he called? I'll Google him. That's it – Bolsonaro. This right-wing genius, this Einstein of politics has got rid of all the laws protecting the Amazon, and declared the whole area open to commercial exploitation.

He's not interested in hiding his ambitions, Mr. Bolsonaro. He's no hypocrite though. On the contrary, he's totally upfront. (I think I'd prefer him to be in charge of this country rather than the hypocrite we have. At least you'd know where you stood.) Thousands and thousands of square kilometres of forest have already been cut down in the Amazon, and thousands and thousands of square kilometres have been burnt down since he came to power (just a year or two ago).

To hell with the natives who have lived in the area for centuries, to hell with the rest of Brazil, to hell with all of South America, and to hell with every corner of the world. Bolsonaro intends to make himself some serious money here. That's how the man must think, if – and it's a big fucking if – he thinks at all.

I doubt you can hear the wildlife in the heart of the Amazon jungle any longer because the chainsaws are making such a racket. To many people this must be a beautiful sound, a masculine sound, the sound of a slot machine jackpot on steroids. If the Amazon forest is our planet's lungs, just listen to them wheeze.

According to Google, Senor – or should I say President – Bolsonaro has five children (one boy just four or five years older than me), so he obviously can't be too concerned about them, isn't losing any sleep over their futures. 'Don't worry, kids, no child of mine is going to be short of oxygen in the future.' He must have shares in an oxygen supply company, that must be it.

But wait, this explains everything: Google says he was educated (sic) – *educated* – at the Army Physical Education School in Rio de Janeiro. Long pause while everyone laughs in disbelief. Hahahaha.

This can't be real. Truly, that's where he went to school – to a physical education establishment. No wonder he's right-wing (who's ever heard of a left-wing military man?) No wonder he hasn't got a brain in his head – though he's doubtless terrific at square-bashing, stomach-crunches and weight-lifting. Doubtless, he will also have been taught to cut back on the empathy for his fellow humans, to strengthen his inclinations towards murdering people rather than caring for them. He's certainly turning out to be the establishment's star pupil, and doubtless they've already got a statue honouring him in the main quadrangle of the Army Physical Education School.

Over twenty per cent of the world's oxygen comes from the Amazon. (Hugh and I spent a lot of time on the internet learning facts like that.) Twenty percent. So how come President B. is allowed to get away with this? Why doesn't the US invade Brazil (they're always super keen to invade other countries, so why the sudden consideration shown to Bolsonaro? Is it an Alliance of Loons)? Stealing other people's oxygen must surely be a crime against humanity? Choking the life out of every-one on the planet is surely genocide? Why is this man, this *inhuman* man, able to get away with potentially murdering millions of people?

He's in a league of his own, this dude. We're talking of death on such a vast scale here, of such unbelievable suffering, he'll likely get away with it – just like Hitler, Stalin and Mao.

If anyone eventually gets Bolsonaro into the International Court in The Hague, which isn't likely, he'll doubtless be 98 years old, in a wheelchair, and, according to his extremely well-paid lawyers, far too unwell to stand trial – as well as being mentally unfit. But then he's mentally unfit *now*, so it can't be possible for him to become even more mentally unfit. I bet he's so crazy, he regularly rushes around his parliament building brandishing burnt branches above his head, shouting, 'How good is this! How good is this!'

These kinds of people drive me nuts. It's their indifference that really gets me. They're utterly selfish, totally narcissistic, and probably psychopaths to boot (I've picked up the lingo from Hugh's parents).

Sam came to see me again yesterday. I always hope you'll meet her, Dr. C, but you never do. You never seem to be around at the same time. Dad's the only one of my family you ever talk to, over the phone, and he's never going to give you my side of the story. Sam might though.

Although she's visited me before, her visits aren't as frequent as I'd like. She says she has too much on. What, lying in bed all morning, and meeting friends in clubs every night? But I only think that. I don't say anything, not wanting to get into one of our arguments in front of the other patients.

We've always been close. Sure, we have our ups and downs – Zoe being one of the downs. I really felt betrayed at the time. I thought me and Zoe were tight, that she was as keen on me as I was on her.

The usual anonymous trolls and flamers were quick to comment on Facebook, but I soon stopped looking or caring. It's toxic, all of that.

But it didn't stop me accusing Zoe of telling everyone about our break-up. I pictured that bunch of giggling girls when she first approached me at the schools' demonstration. All doubtless 'friends' of hers on Facebook. She asked me – with very fake innocence in my opinion – if we had broken up. I wasn't going to knock myself out answering that. She denied telling people. 'Anyway, you don't own me,' she added. Which didn't kind of follow if you ask me.

We didn't speak again until she visited me in here weeks later (when they took Alastair out for a walk in the gardens). I never thought I'd see her again to be honest, so the visit was unexpected. I'm not even sure why she came. The problem was, it suddenly seemed like she was standing on the other side of a huge chasm. I felt we were that far apart.

I accused Sam of spreading the story on social media as well. She denied it of course, and I reluctantly agreed that stealing her younger brother's girlfriend was hardly something she was likely to boast about to her followers. But I'm not sure I trust her – or Zoe.

Sam kind of apologised to me eventually, after days of blocking me out. When she did finally HMU, she said she didn't even fancy Zoe – 'not girls either, to be honest' – but in the next breath accused me of gender bias. Go figure! I think she was trying to say the only reason I was jealous was because my girlfriend had left me for a woman.

'How do you know she's left me?'

'Well, it kinda looks like that, bro.'

'Not necessarily.'

She shrugged. Truth is, Sam made the whole thing even weirder, and made me even more bored by the way the two of them behaved.

I'd respected Zoe, and yes, loved her. I'd waited. Maybe that was my mistake, treating her decently, like a human being.

On this visit, it was like we'd agreed not to go near the subject of Zoe – or that's how it started. She chatted about mum and dad, and about things that were going on in her life (parties, boys). She's never been in the slightest bit interested in current affairs, yet still believes absolutely in every conspiracy theory doing the rounds: the CIA bombed the Twin Towers, the moon landing was a hoax filmed in a Hollywood studio, and so on. So I was sort of surprised when she told me her latest theory. We were sitting by the French windows in the lounge – 'It doesn't smell so bad near the windows.' (Me, I've become used to the permanent cabbage and disinfectant aroma.)

Climate change, she said, is 'a fiction created by Big Business.

'They're making huge profits from manufacturing solar panels, lithium batteries, wind farms and the rest. Even the power stations are in on it, Al. They're either spending vast amounts by converting to clean energy, or by closing down completely – both activities subsidised by taxpayers.'

This little outburst was from someone who normally doesn't give a toss about the climate crisis. I was taken aback.

'Sam,' I said patiently, trying really hard not to roll my eyes, 'global warming has been proven time and time again. You can't just dismiss it out of hand as a conspiracy theory.'

'Scientists have never proven it 100 percent!' She was kind of worked up. 'They receive enormous grants from the Government to do research and write reports, that's why they're all so rich, but they've still not proven anything conclusively.'

'You're saying they're perpetuating a myth? You're kidding!'

She frowned like she was trying hard to follow me, then nodded her head like she suddenly understood.

She changed tack. How could I support the environmentally unsound way that solar panels are manufactured, and how did I personally plan to get rid of them all when they reached the end of their lives in a few years' time – 'Surely you don't want them all to go to landfill, do you, Al?' Touch of sarcasm there, I thought. 'There will be billions of them.'

I had to admit I'd never thought about that. She positively glowed with satisfaction.

She was quoting dad, of course. I realised that pretty quickly, especially when she mentioned that the change in the world's weather in recent years is perfectly natural – a cycle that recurs every few millennia, and it has always been like this. She sounded just like him. He probably put her up to visiting me in the hope of making me see sense. That's how he expresses it: 'Alan, you have to see sense.'

It was probably stupid, but I accused her of taking sides with dad. She denied it vehemently. 'Anyway, you have to stop seeing it as taking sides. It's not a battle, you know.'

'It is with him.'

'Dad really respects your point of view. And he loves you, you know, even though he disagrees with you about this climate business.'

I grunted dismissively.

'He does, Al, he really does.'

I wanted to believe her, but I was all too aware that my family now regarded me as some kind of freak, as an outsider. Dad had even started to call me 'the extinction advocate.' Affectionately, maybe, but it still hurt, especially when Samantha was obviously now taking his side – Sam who always claimed to be completely 'unfazed by' (read 'disinterested in') the fate that was about to befall her, along with everyone else in the world. I've always blamed this on her low mental capacity (which she's happier for me to blame than her looks, which she rates as her number one attribute).

Although indifferent to the recent extreme events of Mother Nature, despite seeing them on the News (or on Facebook) every night, she was unusually generous when I first tried to interest her in our plight.

'Don't worry, Al, I'm sure everything will work out OK.' Unfortunately, she wouldn't, or couldn't, explain why she felt so optimistic.

So now my whole family makes me feel like I don't belong. Inevitable, maybe, when we hold such different opinions. Yet I do appreciate that dad can hardly turn his back on an industry that's employed him ever since he left school, and allowed him to become such a well-known and successful figure. I totally get that, even though I'm sure he wouldn't believe me.

I still hope that one day he'll see the light.

Thinking about dad, reminded me of a cleaner we had when we were young. Maria was from Fiji. She was about twice the size of mum, but still in her twenties.

She was a great hugger (of me and Sam), and always happy. Both of my parents had a problem with the fact she never stopped laughing or talking – especially dad.

'Do you remember Maria?' Sam nodded vaguely. She was a little distracted by two patients having an altercation over a jigsaw puzzle they were assembling at a nearby table.

'They're fine. Ignore them,' I said. 'I don't think I've told you that a few weeks before I ended up in here, dad and I were watching the News, and there was a story about the Government announcing that we wouldn't cut back on burning fossil fuels and that the Pacific Islanders could basically go drown themselves beneath the rising sea levels for all they cared.'

'You're exaggerating, Al.' She sounded exasperated. 'You always exaggerate everything.'

I told her I wasn't exaggerating, and that the Pacific Islanders' situation reminded me of those films we used to watch when we were little, where the hero and heroine are trapped in some cave or other – maybe a room – that's rapidly filling with water. At first, they stand on tiptoes, craning their necks in order to keep their noses above the water. Then they float on their backs, paddling away like mad, until the gap between the rising water and the ceiling is just a centimetre or two, and the viewer's thinking, that's it, this is the end, oh my god they'll drown!

'You always covered your face with a cushion, saying you couldn't bear to watch, and shouted at me to switch channels.' She said she couldn't remember. 'Anyway, at the very last minute, *of course,* one of their friends comes to their rescue – pulls out the plug or whatever.'

I told her that's how it must be for the Islanders. 'They're treading water like crazy, heads just above the surface, but it doesn't look like anyone's going to rescue them. The West has turned its back on their plight, saying in effect, "Tough luck, guys. We're going to continue polluting as before, continue burning fossil fuels, climate change will continue to get worse, and sea levels will continue to rise. Deal with it."'

She was listening to me and, unusually for her, not commenting.

'You know the really awful thing? When the government spokesperson announced they wouldn't do anything to help the Islanders, I couldn't help myself. "That's disgusting," I said. "What are they supposed to do – take to the boats?" I was so, like, indignant.

'And you know what dad said? "We can't afford to cut back on coal mining now that our economy's slowing down, Alan. Jobs depend on it."

'I don't know about that,' I said, 'but Maria lives in Fiji! And she's in danger. What about her?

'"That one will survive," he said – really offhanded – "so don't you worry about her. The Islanders are lazy. She was too, that's why we got rid of her. They're just exaggerating the problem in the hope of getting money off us. If they were sensible, they'd come over here and pick our fruit. Make a bit of money that way. They were happy enough to do that once upon a time, before this global warming nonsense."'

I turned to my sister. I was close to tears. 'I was really upset by that. How could he say such a thing? Maria was lovely, so cool, almost one of the family.'

'Did you say anything to dad?'

'You know what he's like. You can never win an argument with him.'

'I'm sure it wasn't that bad, Al. I think you're imagining how bad it was.'

But I wasn't. That's exactly what happened.

I wondered if Maria had returned to Fiji. I hoped not, even though she always said it was paradise. Poor Maria. If she'd returned home, she'd now be forced to flee, or perish. Supposedly, there will be 200 million climate refugees by the year 2050. I now know one of them.

We sat by the French windows in silence. Sam still had her hand across her nose – I mean, how bad was the smell! – but sometimes took a quick look round the room. (I suspect she held her breath when she did this.) It was obvious, at least to me, that she wasn't really interested in the other patients.

The conversation had dried up – which made me sad, that we had so little to say to each other, that maybe she only visited me in order to spout dad's propaganda.

When she got up to leave, I headed for the exit with her. She stopped near the Reception desk, and suddenly lowered her voice: 'Al, Zoe wanted me to tell you something.' For a split second I was elated, imagining all kinds of wonderful, loving messages from my girl-friend.

'She wants to end it.' She turned away like she didn't care to see the affect her words would have on me. That was unusually sensitive of her, I thought later.

I could scarcely breathe. It must be a mistake. It can't be that – surely not? And it was like Sam could read my mind.

'No, it's nothing to do with me. I told her you'd think that, but it's nothing like that, I promise. We've never seen each other since… since then.'

'What is it then? Why can't she tell me herself?'

'She was scared to. She didn't know how you'd take it. And she couldn't bring herself to text.'

'But why? Why does she want to end it?'

My sister shrugged, briefly hugged me, then walked away. Now both of them had walked away.

But what do they say, don't get mad, get even?

It's the same story everywhere else. The U.S. withdrew from the Paris Agreement because it imposed an 'onerous burden' on their economy. LOL. The Man Who Feels Up Women made that decision. The Twitter doofus ditched that Agreement almost as soon as he got to the Oval Office – doubtless holding up a sheet of paper with his thick spiky signature on it for the cameras, with that look – *See, I can even write my own name!* Such a clever man. No doubt about it!

China is the largest emitter of CO2 *and* the largest coal producer in the world, and the country's run by another psychopath – surprise, surprise. President Xi only does something about pollution when the country's citizens are unable to cycle to work, or even breathe, because of the smog. He's not worried about their welfare, only that they'll be too ill to work.

Europeans increasingly voice their concern about global warming, but as far as I can make out don't take any really serious action. Russia is the largest emitting country that hasn't endorsed the Paris Agreement, and their climate actions have been described by some official body as 'critically insufficient'. Run by another psychopath, of course.

Am I beginning to detect a pattern here?

Australia, like the UK, has a doofus for a leader – not even intelligent enough to be a psychopath. He likes to rush into Parliament with lumps of coal – like a first-footer on Hogmanay – shouting, 'How good is that, how good is that!' Unbelievable but true, and very, very sad (for the rest of us).

Then there's South America. I'm guessing that, apart from Brazil, the continent treats climate change seriously, although most of the countries are too poor to do much about it. Which is also India's argument, home to most of the world's most polluted cities: 'Sorry, boss, love to help out, but things are a little tight right now.'

I always come back to asking myself the same question – and yes, I'm aware that it's a bit of a preoccupation of mine at the moment, Dr. Craig – but how do the leaders of these countries sleep at night? It doesn't seem possible that they're able to. How can they behave in such a way? They're condemning their own kids to an awful future, in fact to a complete lack of any future.

I asked Hugh about this. 'You're being naïve, mate. They can do it because they've always done it. Since the year dot, that's the way it's been. Those who win power just look after themselves and those who helped them get to the top. It won't change.'

'But what about their children?'

'Well, it seems like they don't give a damn about their own kids.' He half laughed. 'Maybe they think of it as some kind of tough love.'

'But why bring them into the world in the first place if you're going to treat them like that? Why not leave them un-born? That's preferable to killing them.'

He didn't have an answer for that. Which is unusual for him.

Benefit of the doubt: it's possible our politicians have our interests at heart, although unlikely. Even though they're morons, they are possibly concerned morons.

Why are they concerned? Because they tell us they are!

Why are they morons? Because the world has always been ruled by morons. No, no, no, that can't be true.

Can it?

Once, they kept caged canaries deep underground in coalmines to warn against the presence of carbon monoxide. That's what I feel like now – a government canary. When I die, everyone will know it's time to leave for another planet.

Zoe's dead. To me, totally dead.

I know what I have to do. It's all that remains for me to do.

When I try to describe the despair that I feel, I only come up with clichéd phrases.

I search for words that will convey the pain in my heart and in my head, but cannot find them in any dictionary.

Blackness. That's not enough.

Despair. That's too weak.

Astronauts always speak of the beauty of our planet when seen from outer space. Our home, they call it, our only home. It strikes each of them, every one of them, when they return to earth, as very precious, like a fragile, newborn plant. They always return home to our world misty-eyed, all of them, without exception.

No wonder. According to the scientists, it's the only planet (out of about 200 billion in our galaxy) that's absolutely perfect, absolutely suited to supporting human life. There aren't any other suitable ones, they say. This is the only one.

Yet we're still intent on trashing it. Destroying it. Despite it being our only home. Despite there not being another house just down the street that we could move into.

Perhaps it's not possible to communicate such horror. The killing of innocent men, women and children. Billions and billions and billions of them. Human extinction. The slaughter of both wild and domesticated animals. The complete annihilation of Mother Nature. Destruction on a truly unimaginable scale…

It's too big to take in, that's the problem. Easier to think of your own family. Try and imagine how bad it will be for them in the future. Mum and Dad, Samantha, granny and grandad, me…

I know it's an inadequate gesture, but I've decided to travel to the capital when I get out of here, to the seat of government. With its grand columns, marbled hallways, imposing statues, spectacular fountains, and eternal flames. With its blind politicians and unthinking bureaucrats.

At the crest of its never-ending steps, beneath the flapping flags, in front of the stern, immobile guards, I will drench myself in my father's lifeblood – the fossil fuel that everyone insists the world cannot do without – and set myself alight.

I will leave a note. In it I will attempt to explain how they have left me no option, left me without any hope.

Just how long do they intend to keep me locked up in here?

Postscript.

I WENT TO VISIT HIM ON THE VERY SAME DAY. THAT DAY, THE tenth of the month. It was during the school holidays, so I wasn't in my usual rush.

It was grey and overcast, and there was an icy wind. The garden was bleak and without any colour. When I walked into the clinic, I immediately sensed the barely suppressed air of excitement. Patients were standing together in small groups talking. Despite looking a little furtive, and many of them having their mouths open, they presented an unusually sane demeanour. It was their eyes that gave them away. They darted this way and that, as if looking for a way out, or perhaps hoping to be rescued from the situation in which they found themselves.

I scarcely paid any attention to these groups of whispering patients to be honest, being too caught up thinking about what Alan and I were going to talk about. I approached the reception desk, and asked if I could see him. It was only at that moment that I became alarmed. The young nurse – whom I knew a little – turned to a colleague as if seeking help. It was obvious to me that she was panicked. The colleague – whom I also recognised – invited me into a small office adjoining the reception area. There, he broke the news.

After his initial statement, I scarcely heard anything

he said, but perhaps because I was known as a regular visitor and a good friend of Alan's, I was allowed to remain at the clinic for about an hour – in fact, until his parents arrived. During that time I spoke to many staff members, as well as to some of the patients. I even had a brief word with Dr. Craig. He appeared quite shattered. Slowly, I formed a picture of what had happened.

Because of the cold, it seems there were few patients out in the garden during the mid-morning break, so there was just one carer in attendance.

At least one patient noticed Alan go to the shed where the hospital stored the gardening equipment, but no one thought anything of it. A little later my friend was seen crossing the lawn with a can of petrol. He dragged the bench further away from the old oak tree before sitting down. Then he upended the can to douse himself with fuel. 'There was a lot of it,' another patient told me. 'Must have been a full can, I reckon.' And he set himself alight.

I gather it happened as quickly as that.

The few patients who were outside, watched from a distance, although one or two of them did edge tentatively closer to the blaze. Most were silent, some, from what I understand, jumped up and down with excitement. Alastair was one of those. He was *doing his thing* – which I only mention because both of us regarded him as a bit of a character, and because I don't believe it would have bothered Alan in the slightest. Most likely, he'd have found it funny. One patient was applauding.

The carer was a newcomer to the home, a junior nurse. When she noticed the cluster of patients, she walked towards them to find out what was going on – more inquisitive than worried at that stage.

She described Alan as resembling 'a flaming torch, the flesh of his face melting like wax on a candle'. It's a description that still haunts me. She told Dr. Craig that he made no sound, but the flames, whipped almost horizontal by the strong wind, made a faint rushing, crackling noise.

She ran to the house, screaming for help. 'She was quite hysterical,' another staff member told me – 'understandably.' Fortunately for my friend a few minutes elapsed before a couple of nurses reached him with fire extinguishers. I say 'fortunately' because I know he would not have wanted to survive with such terrible burns.

By the time the fire was extinguished, he was declared dead.

My friend never made it to the capital. Dr. Craig was still refusing to allow him to leave the clinic, and he wasn't prepared to wait until he was released to make his protest, having no idea how long that might be. It meant that his death didn't receive the publicity it would have received if he'd killed himself in front of the Parliament. That had been his dream – maximum publicity for his cause, our cause.

Most of the national newspapers carried a short article on the self-immolation of an inmate in a mental facility – about the same length as for someone killed in a car crash.

No one had taken a photograph (thank goodness), and as a result the Press weren't that interested. Perhaps they thought that kind of thing went on all the time in mental institutions. Only *The Guardian* reported that Alan had killed himself due to frustration at the lack of progress in his country over climate change.

A Greens' senator stated in the chamber that it was a national tragedy, and hoped that the Government would finally introduce legislation to deal with global warming before others copied this tragic incident.

I see Alan's death as a sign of hope. I believe it shows that people are becoming increasingly aware of how the system is rigged, and how the worst polluters have the most influence over government. They're realizing that oil, coal and gas companies actively contaminate the democratic process by spending vast amounts of money attacking irrefutable climate science and environmental research. All they're interested in is profits.

As Greta Thunberg says: 'We need to change the rules.' Rules are laws, and now it's time for laws to be introduced that put people and the environment first, before everything else, especially profits. It's as simple as that.

There are other positive signs: investors are moving away from the fossil fuel companies in droves. And Covid-19 has shown us that the world is now truly global. There are no borders, no parties and no vested interests when it comes to either viruses or climate change. We really are all in this together.

In a short note left for Dr. Craig, my friend said that he was sorry he did what he did, but explained that he carried it out because of the lack of progress in dealing with global warming. 'I'm not mad, and my actions have nothing to do with my treatment here.' There was no message left for his family. Nevertheless, his action had a profound effect on at least one person – a most surprising one: his father.

A few months later, John Cunliffe resigned from his position as CEO of the international oil company, making an impassioned speech about the dangers of fossil fuels for the future of mankind, and the immorality of us continuing to use them. He then spent an intensive few weeks being interviewed by most of the leading television stations and newspapers in the country (an ordeal he confessed to undergoing solely on behalf of his dead son).

He also sold the city's family mansion, and went with his wife to live in the country. (Samantha refused to accompany them – 'I gather there's no nightlife in Woop Woop,' Mr. Cunliffe told me with a smile.) I know Alan would have been extremely proud of his father, and of his own part in bringing about such a 'conversion'.

The diary – if that's what it was – which Alan wrote for Dr. Craig, he left to me. It was placed in an envelope and addressed, *Private and Confidential*. I don't believe it would otherwise have been given to me by a young nurse when I paid my ill-timed visit to Alan on the very day that he killed himself.

I'm publishing it now because I think it deserves to be published. Because I received permission to do so from Mr. and Mrs. Cunliffe. Because I think Alan would have agreed that it was the right thing to do. Because all proceeds will go to the Foundation set up in his name. And because, unbelievably, within weeks of his death, the government was still proposing legislation that would have a detrimental effect on the environment.

This time it was to allow companies to open new coalmines without considering their climate risk, and with no responsibility for the downstream emissions or the harm those emissions might cause to people and the environment. There are doubtless other pieces of legislation in the pipeline along similar lines, so it is up to all of us to continue to fight such idiocy.

When one reads about such laws, it really does make one despair. Such stupidity, irresponsibility and blatant greed makes one want to give up. With the world still reeling from the Covid-19 pandemic, concerns about global warming have been relegated by governments to the back burner, with all efforts being aimed at economic recovery, to returning life to normal. This is lunacy.

My friend died in the early days of the pandemic, before it became really serious. He never witnessed the time when people could talk of nothing else. But some are already beginning to understand that Covid-19 will be a mere blip in history when compared to the catastrophic impact of global warming. Unlike the corona virus, climate change will affect every man, woman and child on the planet, without exception, and sanctuary through self-isolation will not be an option.

Anyone who survives this looming climate catastrophe will be back living in the Dark Ages.

I'm hoping that my friend's short book might achieve what his suicide seemingly failed to achieve. In the words of the Alan Cunliffe Foundation: 'Action on Climate Change Today. Or there will be no Tomorrow.'

Hugh Gosling. June 2020.

ACKNOWLEDGEMENTS

I would like to thank those who have read and commented on this novella, but especially Bryan Keon-Cohen, Alex Fenton and Monica Sidaway. Also, the many authors, scientists, researchers and ordinary men and women who have never given up trying to make the world aware of the lack of time that remains for us to do something about the climate crisis. But especially my wife, Elizabeth, who continues to make everything possible. Thank you to all.

www.ingramcontent.com/pod-product-compliance
Lightning Source LLC
Chambersburg PA
CBHW030434120726
47903CB00003B/955